WARNING

This book contains scenes of intense violence and some disturbing themes. Some parts of this book may be considered violent, cruel, disturbing, or unusual. This book is *not* intended for those easily offended or appalled. Please enjoy at your own discretion.

CW01499354

Table of Contents

Lovelorn

Jon Athan

For more information on this book or the author, please visit www.jon-athan.com. General inquiries are welcome.

Facebook:
https://www.facebook.com/AuthorJonAthan
Twitter: @Jonny_Athan
Instagram: @AuthorJonnyAthan
Email: info@jon-athan.com

Book cover by Sean Lowery:
http://indieauthordesign.com/

Thank you for the support!

ISBN: 9798636424000

First Edition

Chapter One

Lovelorn

Lovelorn: unhappy because of unrequited love.

"I thought you loved me," Benjamin Crawford said, his voice breaking like a young, embarrassed teenager's.

He was twenty-four years old, tall and lean. He wore a beanie every day to hide his thinning black hair and receding hairline. The hat was practically stitched to his scalp. His large, dark pupils—ringed with dim blue irises—revealed his depression and spoke volumes about his insecurities. And his insecurities turned into voices in his head.

One voice said: *she never loved you*.

Another voice said: *no one could love a balding faggot like you*.

The sides of his mouth twitched as he tried to force a smile. He lost that battle. His eyes welled with tears and his lips sank into a frown.

He asked, "You love me, don't you?"

Eighteen-year-old Madison Murphy stood before him. She was known as a social media influencer, although many referred to her as an 'e-girl' due to her style. She had brown hair with gray streaks, her bangs reaching down to her eyebrows. She wore a black tube top under a large flannel shirt, tight jeans, and Doc Martens. She was about a foot shorter than Benjamin, but she was one spunky kid.

She established a following by posting provocative pictures and edgy memes on the internet. People—mostly men—were attracted to her youth and her appearance.

She leaned against the back of Benjamin's black SUV. She shook her head and narrowed her bloodshot eyes to slits. She had smoked a bowl of marijuana earlier in the night, so she was still high. She glanced around. They were in a wooded area, illuminated by the stars and the red glow of the SUV's blinking hazard lights. She could see a tall office building to her left, but all of the lights were off inside.

She asked, "What time is it?"

"Answer the question, Madison."

"What question?"

"Do you love me?"

Madison turned her head to the side and said, "Come on, Benny, I don't want to talk about that stuff. This was supposed to be, like, a chill night, remember?" She beckoned to him and said, "Come on, take me home. I wanna sleep already. I got so–"

"We're not going anywhere until we talk about this," Benjamin interrupted. Tears dripped from his eyes as he blinked. He said, "You can't... You can't *drag* me along forever. I need you to tell me the truth. I need... I... I need the fucking truth, Madison! Do you love me? Yes or no?"

Madison lowered her head, made an 'O' with her lips, then blew out loudly in disappointment. She had no idea what he was talking about. Love? She never professed her love to him. They never had sex before. She kissed him on the cheek a couple of times, but those were nothing more than friendly pecks. She treated him like a close friend or an older brother.

She said, "The truth is: I *don't* love you, Benny."

Benjamin grimaced and staggered, as if he had just been hit in the gut with a sledgehammer. His tears cascaded across his rosy cheeks—*endless.*

Madison smiled nervously and said, "Benny, come on. I don't love you, but that... that doesn't mean anything. We're friends. We're *good* friends. I care about you. And I trust you, you know? You're not an asshole like those other guys."

"Like... Like that guy you... that guy you kissed at the concert? That... That fucking Chad?"

"Chad?" Madison repeated, giggling. "Who the hell is Chad? His name was Michael and we were just–"

"I *don't* want to know his fucking name!"

Madison hopped and gasped, startled by Benjamin's shout. She stepped back until she crashed into the SUV. They stood in a tense silence. It was as if the wind had stopped blowing and the trees had stopped rustling. Madison saw a feral, desperate look in Benjamin's eyes. He resembled a man fighting for survival.

But no one was threatening him.

Madison said, "Benjamin, you're scaring me."

"Did you know Michael before we went to the concert?"

"Wha–What?"

"Did you know him? Did you invite him there? Because he looked like he knew you, Madison."

Madison stuttered, "S–So what? Wha–What are you trying to say?"

Benjamin approached her. Madison sprawled herself out against the SUV's rear hatch, arms outstretched. They stood less than a yard away from each other.

Benjamin wagged his finger at her and asked, "How many guys have you been seeing behind my back? Huh? Are you fucking them? Did you... Oh God, someone else has been orbiting you, right? You fell in love with *him,* didn't you? What? Huh? What?! He looked better than me?!" He took off his beanie and yelled, "He has better hair than me?! Is that it?!"

"Oh my God," Madison whimpered.

She was crying now, too. She looked to her left, then her right. Benjamin was too close, so she couldn't escape.

She stuttered, "Ben–Benny, what is going–"

"You've been using me, haven't you?"

"Using you? Are you crazy?"

"It's true. You used me for rides to school and the mall. You treated me like a... like a fucking... a chauffeur or whatever you call 'em. You smoked my weed and drank my beer with your friends. I lent you money. I bought you presents, Madison. I bought you jewelry from fucking Tiffany and clothes from Burberry. I spent so much fucking money on you."

"Hey. *Hey,* my love isn't for sale," Madison snapped, puffy-eyed. "I'm not some hooker, okay? You gave me those gifts because... because... You said it was because we were good friends. Those were your words. And that's what we are, Benjamin: Good. *Friends.* And this... this isn't how friends treat each other. This is scary, bro. I'm, like... I'm shook right now."

Benjamin heard the fear in her voice. He saw his reflection on the rear window with each blink of the hazard lights. He looked like a large, warped shadow in the red glow. He didn't realize he was shaking until he glanced at his hand. He was blinded by his rage. He almost lost control of himself. He lowered his hand and drew a sharp breath.

Madison breathed a shaky sigh of relief. Her arms fell to her sides. She thought about sidestepping away from him, but she didn't want to aggravate the situation. *Do what he says and everything will be fine,* she thought.

Benjamin said, "Yeah, um… I'm sorry."

"It–It's okay. I get it. It was just a misunderstanding."

"Yeah, but… I need to know something, Madison. Do I… Ah, shit, do I have a chance with you?"

"A chance with me?"

"You know what I mean. You said we're good friends, so maybe we can be something *more.* I'm not talking about right now, but, like, in the future, you know? Do I have a chance to get with you?"

Yes—it was a lie, but Madison believed it would have ended the conversation and led to her safe return home. But she didn't want to string him along. She liked him because of his taste in music and movies as well as his sense of humor. She wasn't attracted to him, though, and she was afraid of him because of his recent outbursts. They weren't dating, but he was already jealous and obsessive.

Benjamin was dangerous and unhinged. Madison was young, she didn't have a lot of experience in dating, but even she could see that.

She said, "I'll walk home or catch an Uber. Good night, Benny."

Benjamin pressed his knuckles against her chest and pushed her back against the rear hatch. He pinned her to the SUV and glared at her. Pupils dilated with fear, Madison looked at his fist, then at his angry eyes, and then at his fist again. Her breathing intensified as she tried to squirm away, but his knuckles were buried in her soft flesh.

"Do I have a chance to get with you?" Benjamin repeated.

Madison choked down the lump in her throat with one loud gulp. Tragic news headlines flooded her mind: *teen beheads girlfriend in a jealous rage; teenage girl shot and killed by ex-boyfriend; Instagram influencer found dead in a suitcase.* Things like that— shootings, stabbings, beheadings—were supposed to happen to other people in other parts of the world.

She never thought it would happen to her. She saw herself as a harmless, innocent eighteen-year-old girl. She never intentionally hurt anyone. She wasn't manipulative or aggressive. She didn't bully her peers. She was only trying to live life to the fullest. *Why would anyone want to hurt someone like me?*— she thought.

In Benjamin's eyes, she saw the evil of humanity for the first time in her young life. She stood in the presence of an unhinged killer. *Yes, no, maybe*—her vocabulary was deleted. She couldn't say a word.

Through his gritted teeth, Benjamin hissed, "I knew it. You *were* trying to trick me. You're always tricking me. You–You manipulate guys like me to get what you want. Then you act like the victim when guys *take* what they want from you. When we take what you promised! *What we deserve!* You're just like all of the other *bitches* out there, Madison! You're a cunt! You're all cunts! Selfish, stupid, ugly, fake, disgusting cunts!"

He swung his other fist at Madison's face, but he stopped before he could make contact. Madison gasped and recoiled in fear. She ducked and squeezed out of Benjamin's grip. She crawled out from under him on all fours. Benjamin screamed in frustration as he punched the rear window—left, right, left, *right*. The SUV wobbled with each blow. His knuckles cracked while the window remained unblemished.

"Oh my God," Madison whimpered.

She struggled to her feet. Hands and knees stained with mud, she hurried away from the SUV. She walked, albeit quickly, because she didn't want to arouse any suspicion. She believed she could sneak away.

From the SUV, Benjamin barked, "Madison! Madison, don't leave! Don't you fucking leave me, you bitch!"

"Leave me alone!" Madison cried out without looking back. She panted in short, desperate breaths. She whispered, "Please don't follow me, please don't follow me, please don't follow me."

A gust of wind rushed through the woods, hurling dirt, leaves, and branches towards the SUV. The tree branches creaked and groaned while the leaves rustled. The engine of a car roared on a road beyond the trees, followed by another humming engine. The tense silence in the woods was replaced by chaos, matching the confusion and disarray in Madison's mind. She couldn't concentrate.

Her eyes widened as she heard the rapid footsteps behind her. She didn't have the opportunity to turn around. *Thud!* Her vision went black, her body stiffened up, and she fell forward. She landed face-first in the mud. Blood leaked out of a gash on the back of her head, dying her gray streaks red. The moist mud bubbled around her head as she struggled to breathe.

Benjamin stood behind her, carrying a large, jagged stone in his hands. He stood motionless for a minute, ashen-faced and wide-eyed. His face said something along the lines of: *what the hell did I just do?* His mind had been plagued with violent thoughts since he was a child. For years, he fantasized about hurting the people who hurt him. But he never went through with it.

The stone landed in the mud between his feet. He dug his muddy fingers into his thin hair and stepped back.

"No, no, no," he muttered. "What did I do? What... What do I do now? Fuck, oh fuck, Madison... Madison, I'm sorry. Please say something. Hey, come on, say some... *Fuck!*"

He grabbed her shoulder and rolled her onto her back. She tilted her head back and jutted her chin out repeatedly, as if she were about to cough up a hairball. Her lips fluttered and the mud spurted away from her face as she hacked and gasped for air. Thin slits of her red sclerae were visible through her narrowed eyelids. Her eyes were rolling back.

Benjamin grabbed Madison's legs and dragged her back to the SUV. He found some comfort in the hazard lights. The red glow made it harder for him to see the blood trickling out of her scalp. He opened the rear hatch, then he slammed it shut. Trunks were used for cargo and dead bodies, but he wasn't ready to accept the severity of Madison's wound. He didn't want to transport her in his trunk and dump her body somewhere like a serial killer. He wanted to save her.

So, he ran to the side of the SUV and opened the passenger door instead. Living people rode shotgun after all. Then he ran back to the rear of the SUV.

"Oh shit," he muttered as he slid to a stop. He tugged on his hair and screamed, "No! No! Shit! This can't be happening! Please, no!"

Madison convulsed on the ground. Saliva and mud frothed on her mouth. She gritted her teeth until the enamel cracked and her gums bled. She let out slow, pained groans, chest rising and falling rapidly as she panicked. Fists clenched and toes curled, her limbs trembled uncontrollably. She went into shock due to her serious brain trauma.

Sobbing between every word, Benjamin rubbed his face with both hands and said, "I'm… sorry. Madison… no… God… why? No… No… please."

He threw a flurry of jabs at the rear window. He scuffed the window while shattering his knuckles. He felt the burning pain across his hands and forearms, but he couldn't tame his fury. He was angry at Madison, himself, and the world. The violent thoughts invaded his mind once again. Violence caused the problem, so violence could solve it.

"You brought this on yourself," he whispered as he took a pocket-knife out of his back pocket.

He opened it with a flick of his wrist. A serrated three-inch blade snapped out of the handle. His hand trembled—partly due to his broken bones, partly due to his fear. He crouched beside Madison. She had stopped shaking, but her head continued to roll from side to side. She didn't open her eyes, but she clung to life. She wasn't ready to die.

She didn't have much of a choice, though.

Tears dripping with each blink, voice trembling, Benjamin said, "I told you everything about me. I bought you clothes and jewelry and perfume because... because I loved seeing you happy. Your smile was so cute, so beautiful. I want to see you smile again. After everything I did for you, you can at least give me that, can't you?"

Benjamin's voice sounded muffled in Madison's ears. She couldn't remember how she ended up on the ground. She couldn't remember the concert earlier that night or her kiss with Michael. Distorted images from her past flashed in her mind—shattered memories. She thought about her mother, her father, and her older sister.

Benjamin grabbed her chin and forced the blade into Madison's mouth. He sawed into her left cheek, starting at the corner of her mouth and stopping near her ear. And he wiggled the blade every inch of the way to widen the wound. Her cheek collapsed into her mouth as two flaps of flesh. The blood from her soft tissue stained her teeth, but some white from her pearly enamel was still visible.

Madison coughed as drops of blood hit the back of her throat. Some blood flowed into her ear canal, too, further damaging her hearing.

Benjamin repeated his actions on her right cheek. Due to Madison's coughing, the blade zigzagged across her cheek. The flaps blew *away* from her face as she wheezed. The blade had also sliced into her tongue. The inside of her mouth was red—*blood-red*. He carved a Glasgow smile onto her face. It didn't bring any joy to him.

Face caked with mud and painted with blood, cheeks cut open and mutilated, he couldn't find her beauty now. Her heavenly luster was gone.

He said, "I'm sorry, Maddie, but you made me do this. You… You bitch!"

He thrust the blade into the side of Madison's neck. He pulled it in and out, slowly sawing into her throat. A three-inch blade could only get him so far. He pushed the blade as deep as possible with each thrust. He felt some resistance as he cut through her firm muscles. It was a bloody mess, and it only got bloodier as he severed her jugular. The blood shot out in geysers.

One.

Two.

Three.

Four long squirts.

The blood turned the mud under her body into a patch of red sludge. He lost his grip on the handle a few times because of the blood, too. He scraped her spine, but he couldn't snap it at that angle. There wasn't enough space in the manmade crevice on her neck. He cut her Adam's apple in half, severed her trachea, and sliced into her esophagus. He reached the center of her neck, but he couldn't tolerate the pain in his hand anymore.

Beheadings were tiring. The terrorists just made it look easy.

He sat beside her and caught his breath while waving his hands as if he had just touched a hot pan. With the sun rising beyond the trees, casting rays of dark orange sunshine on them, he could see inside the wound on Madison's neck. He saw red, some white, and even tints of blue and purple. *Bloody flesh, sturdy bones, and severed veins?*—he thought. The blood was so plentiful that he could catch a whiff of its metallic scent.

He looked at Madison's muddy face. Her eyes were now closed. Wet *crackling* sounds escaped her mouth and the wound on her neck. She stopped moving during the attempted beheading. She passed away after her jugular was severed. The loss of blood and the shock killed her. And Benjamin didn't notice until that very moment. He tried to speak, but his words were replaced by croaks and groans. His quivering lips sent droplets of saliva into the air.

He slapped himself and shouted, "No! Don't fucking cry for her! Don't be a pussy, man! Don't be a cuck! Don't be..."

His voice broke again. He covered his face and sobbed. Then he slapped himself again—once, twice, *thrice*. Cheeks flushed, he growled at Madison.

He barked, "No! You're not going to win! *You* cheated on *me,* you whore! *You* are the bad guy! *You* deserve this!"

He grabbed her head in one hand and thrust the blade into her neck with the other. His hands and sleeves were drenched in blood. His knuckles and palm stung because of his broken bones, but his adrenaline protected him. He sawed into her neck for another thirty minutes. He couldn't break her cervical vertebrae, though. Her head was barely attached to her body by some skin and muscle.

As he dug through her flannel pockets, Benjamin muttered, "You think you're a star, huh? You're a fucking celebrity, *huh?* I'll make you a star, you cheating bitch. Yeah, I'll make you the biggest, *bloodiest* star in the world..."

He took her cell phone out of her pocket. He tried to unlock it using her right index finger and the fingerprint sensor on the back of her phone. A message popped up: *No match*. He wiped her finger clean, then he cleaned the sensor. He tried it again and—*voila!*—the phone unlocked. He stood up with his legs shaking under him. He photographed her body from every angle. He zoomed in on her butchered neck for one of the pictures.

As he scrolled through her contact list, he whispered, "Michael, right? Let's see how Michael likes this."

He found two Michaels in her contact list. He sent them all of the pictures. Chuckling and crying, he sent the pictures to the contacts labeled 'Mommy' and 'Daddy,' too. He opened her web browser and visited several websites. He logged in to a Discord server for users to chat about 'e-girls' and share their lewd pictures. He uploaded the pictures of Madison's corpse to the chat site. Then he posted the photos on a forum for incels—*involuntary celibates*. He uploaded the pictures to several random subreddits, too.

He tapped his way to Madison's Instagram app. She had 35,000 followers. He posted a picture of her corpse as an Instagram Story. Then he typed out a text post for another Instagram Story.

He read the post aloud as he typed each word: "My name is Benjamin Crawford. You saw me on Maddie's Stories before. I killed her because she cheated on me. This is what happens when you cheat." He uploaded another picture as an Instagram Story, then he typed out another one. He said, "All women are the same. Selfish animals. Fucking cancer to mankind. Kill them *ALL!* Fuck you *ALL!*"

He staggered back until he crashed into the rear hatch of the SUV. The phone landed in the mud between his feet and Madison's. It buzzed as she received messages from her followers. He held the knife up to his wrist. He nicked himself because of his trembling hand. His vision blurred because of his tears.

I have to do this, he told himself. *There's no other way out. You can't run. You confessed already. Come on, you can do it!*

He cut his wrist horizontally. The cut was thin, but it still stung and bled. The blood rolled across his palm. He cut himself again. The parallel cut, directly above the other, was deeper. More blood oozed out of the second wound, but he didn't cut an artery. He cut himself a third time, closer to the center of his forearm.

He leaned back against the rear hatch, then he slid down until he sat on the bumper. A tingly sensation spread through his hand, then his fingers turned cold. But he didn't feel like he was dying. He plunged the blade into his forearm, stabbing himself seven times. He cracked his bones with some of the stabbings, too. His arm was covered in blood. The warm liquid dripped from his fingertips.

He wasn't bleeding nearly as much as Madison, though. He sawed into his other wrist, cutting through the veins and scraping at his bones, but he grew tired after a few seconds. The loss of blood took a toll on his arm. He could barely hold the knife in his cold, pale hand. So, he held the knife in both hands and stretched his arms out in front of him with the blade pointing at his chest.

He screamed as he tried to stab himself through the heart. He cut through his shirt and skin, but he couldn't break his sternum.

At his feet, the phone buzzed. In less than ten minutes, Madison had received several messages from her mother and one of the Michaels as well as dozens of her Instagram followers. There was even one missed call.

Michael wrote: *yo, what the hell is this? A prank?*

Madison's mother sent: *Maddie, wtf?? Is it makeup?*

One follower sent: *fucking awesome, dude! How much did the makeup cost and how long did it take?*

Another follower wrote: *this is just disgusting. What the hell is wrong with you? Attention whore…*

Then the phone started vibrating in the mud. Madison's mom was calling again. The pictures looked too real.

"Die, ju–just let me die," Benjamin mumbled.

He stabbed himself in the chest again. He cut into his pectoral muscle—a flesh wound. He thrust the blade at his stomach, but he stopped before he could stab himself. *Not in the stomach,* he thought, *they always say that's too painful on TV.* He stabbed himself in the chest a third time. Once again, he missed his sternum and stabbed his other pectoral muscle.

He looked up upon hearing the wailing sirens. A police cruiser raced towards his SUV, following the dirt path. He glanced over his shoulder. He couldn't see through the rear window, but he heard another police cruiser on the other side of the vehicle. He was surrounded by cops. He leaned forward and grabbed the phone.

On Madison's Instagram account, he posted another update: *It's almost over. I'm going out in a blaze of glory, bitches.*

The phone slipped out of his hands as a vehicle skidded to a stop in front of him. The sirens wailed again, then the car doors swung open. A male cop hopped out of the driver's seat, a female cop jumped out of the passenger seat. They took cover behind the doors and aimed their pistols at the SUV.

The man yelled, "Put the knife down! Put it down!"

"Drop the weapon!" the woman demanded.

Benjamin heard another police cruiser stopping on the other side of the SUV. The scene fell into disharmony as the cops yelled at each other.

Crossfire!

Crossfire!

Crossfire!

Benjamin covered his mouth with one hand as he broke down. Death was scarier when thinking was involved. He thought about the pain—*am I going to feel anything? Does it hurt?*—then he thought about the afterlife—*does Heaven exist? Am I going to hell? Is it all going to go black?* But he preferred death to prison. He didn't want to live a life of shame and celibacy.

Eyes stuck on Madison's face, he thrust the knife into his own neck. He clenched his teeth and grimaced. Blood spurted out as he moved the blade in his neck. He failed to sever his jugular, though. He saw a cop rushing towards him. He pulled the knife out, then he stabbed himself again. Blood squirted onto the rear window and dribbled down his throat.

But he missed his jugular again.

He pulled the blade out once more. He thrust it at his neck again, but before he could cut himself, the cop grabbed his arm and threw him onto the ground. The cop disarmed him in one swift move. He stopped before he could roll Benjamin onto his back. The wounds on his neck were deep and grotesque, and his arms were mutilated. Instead of handcuffing him, he placed some light pressure on his neck—enough to slow the bleeding but not enough to suffocate him.

The cop yelled, "We need first-aid over here!"

"N–No," Benjamin said in a voice weaker than a whisper. The cops couldn't hear him over the chaos in the woods. He croaked out, "N–No, no... le–let me die. N–No, don't... stop it... pl–please..."

The cops raced to save him. He was destined to suffer for the rest of his life. And, depending on the prison, his celibacy was on the menu for many angry prisoners.

Chapter Two

Stood Up

Micah Watson sat at a booth in a diner—*Mario's Diner*. He read about Benjamin and Madison on his MacBook Air while sipping on some coffee from a mug.

The article, from a mainstream news outlet, reported the tragedy without hesitation. It linked to other articles titled: *5 Things to Know About Benjamin Crawford, the Social Media Killer* and *5 Things to Know About Madison Murphy*. Madison didn't get an extravagant headline because she wasn't the star of the show. Yet, it felt like the articles were written with her blood.

The journalists reported Benjamin's online exploits, discussing the existence of Madison's pictures and describing them in great detail. They posted the sources, too—*'The images spread like wildfire, posted on Discord, Facebook, Instagram, Twitter, and practically every social media site on the internet.'* It was almost as if they were nudging their audiences into looking for them.

And it worked.

Micah's curiosity got the best of him. He was fascinated by the crime. Like most people, whether they admitted it or not, he was interested in the macabre. Humans were mesmerized by blood and enchanted by the frailty of life. Car accidents led to rubbernecking drivers and burning houses attracted neighbors from the entire neighborhood. One person's tragedy was another's entertainment.

On Google, Micah searched: *"Madison Murphy" pictures*. News articles occupied the top search results. Then he stumbled upon a forum. It was a forum dedicated to involuntary celibates. *Incels*—he didn't know much about them, but he had read the term a few times on the news. They were blamed for many acts of public violence.

He was only there for the pictures, though. He scrolled through a thread until he found one—a picture of the poor girl's corpse. He sneered in disgust, then his cheeks inflated. He stopped himself from spitting out his coffee. It was more grotesque than he had imagined. It was one of the worst images of death he had ever seen.

He looked away and scrolled past the other pictures. He was nauseous because of the violence, but he was still interested in the crime. He read some of the comments.

A user named 'Solo22' wrote: *yassss, king! Benny's a hero!*

Another user named 'CancerCel' wrote: *that's what she gets for liking Charlie's Angels lol* (He was referencing the 2019 Charlie's Angels reboot and a post Madison made about the movie before her death. She enjoyed it quite a bit.)

Some of the members expressed disgust and sadness. Others attempted to one-up each other in hopes of posting the darkest, edgiest comment. They loved the attention. The community was split. Half of the users believed Madison deserved to die and hailed Benjamin as a hero, the other half believed

Madison was innocent and Benjamin's actions only served to further damage their image.

"Holy shit," Micah whispered. "What's wrong with these people?"

He hopped upon seeing the shadow of a person at the booth behind him. The other diner stood up and threw some cash on the table to cover his bill. As he walked past him, the older gentleman gave Micah a look of disgust. Yet, he shared the blame for looking at Micah's monitor and catching a glimpse of the gore in the first place.

Micah slammed his MacBook shut, then he leaned back and scratched his curly black hair. The sides of his mouth twitched as he forced a smile.

He stuttered, "I–I'm sorry, sir. It's just research for a project. I–I'm a writer, you know?"

The man kept walking and sneering. Micah glanced around the restaurant. There was a family at another booth, but they couldn't see his monitor from their table. There were a few people at the bar to his right. They sat with their backs to him. He opened his MacBook again and closed the tab before anyone else could see it. He looked around the diner again.

He muttered, "Ahh, damn it. Why did I search that here? Maybe I'm just as crazy as those other guys..."

The door chime rang. An elderly couple hobbled into the diner. A peppy woman with curly crimson hair greeted them at the door. The chatter in the diner was loud. Everyone was talking to someone. The scent of crisp bacon and pungent coffee wafted through the restaurant. The morning sunshine bathed the diners at the booths with a pleasant warmth. It was a regular, peaceful day.

Micah pulled his cell phone out of his pocket. He browsed through his collection of dating apps. To his dismay, he didn't receive any messages or 'likes' on any of his profiles. He was honest and consistent in all of his accounts, too—twenty-six years old, five-foot-eleven, 160 pounds, Virgo, no smoking, some drinking, and non-religious. He described himself as a part-time deliveryman for a local pizza joint and a part-time author. He self-published fantasy and horror novels during his spare time.

His profile picture depicted him smiling at his bathroom mirror. He wore a button-up shirt for the picture, and he styled his hair with wax. His smile was wide and toothy—awkward and unnatural. He wasn't an ugly man, he wasn't Quasimodo, but he lacked confidence. There were some pitted acne scars on his cheeks, so he used a filter on his pictures—and it was painfully obvious. Across all of his accounts, his username read: *MicahW94*.

He opened a message thread with a woman named Karla Lopez. Her username read: *Karla99.* She was twenty-one years old. According to her profile, she loved pizza, she enjoyed reading, she was struck with wanderlust, and she was looking for a serious relationship. They shared some conversations, but Micah didn't ask her out on a date. He was waiting for the perfect opportunity, but he waited so long that his time had run out. She stopped responding.

He sent her eight messages on eight different days. She didn't read any of them. In the dating world, it was called 'ghosting.'

Hey, how was your sleep?

What's your plan for today?

How's it going?

Good morning! Sleep well?

Hello?

I'm going to catch a movie this weekend. What are you doing?

Karla, you okay?

Hello??

Micah sighed in disappointment as he read the messages. He looked through his other conversations with women. They all ended the same—*ghosted*. He opened his most recent conversation with a user named *Lovebird95*. She introduced herself as Natalie Cano. She claimed to be a travel guide and vlogger, a law student, independent model, and an entrepreneur. Her pictures showed a curvy brunette woman in tight dresses and tiny bikinis.

In their conversations, they spoke about traveling, movies, music, and books. Most of Natalie's words sounded overly formal and robotic, as if she were copying sentences from Wikipedia and other websites. She was kind and affectionate, though. She showered Micah with compliments and often teased him with dirty talk. She sent him 'naughty' pictures, too, but she refused to call him. *I live with my grandma to take care of her, I don't want to bother her,* she claimed.

Micah sent her three messages that morning.

At 7:45 AM: *Good morning, Nat! I'm getting ready to go to the diner now. How was your sleep?* It was followed by a kissing emoji.

At 8:52 AM: *Okay, I'm here. Can't wait to finally meet you. A little nervous, to be honest.* It was followed by a laughing emoji with tears of joy.

At 9:45 AM: *Are you okay? You said at 9, right? Everything okay? Should I call you?*

The clock on his phone now read: *10:23 AM.* They were supposed to meet at the diner at nine o'clock in the morning for a breakfast date. He thought about sending her another message, but he didn't want to sound clingy. *Maybe she went to the wrong diner, maybe she's having car trouble, maybe something happened to her grandma,* he thought.

He read their previous messages, eyes glued to the screen like a lonely housewife reading a romance novel on a Kindle. Natalie always rejected Micah's requests to call or video chat. She refused to leave voice messages, too. It was either too loud or too quiet whenever Micah asked to hear her voice. She claimed she lived in Ventura, California, about an hour away from his hometown depending on the traffic.

She requested money from Micah so she could drive to his neighborhood and rent a hotel room nearby. She insisted on renting a hotel because she wanted to spend the weekend with Micah without driving back and forth, and she didn't want to stay at Micah's home because she claimed she wasn't the type to sleep with a man on the first night. She told Micah she was a virgin, and she was saving her virginity for someone special.

'I want my first time to be with the right guy... someone like you, maybe,' she wrote in a message riddled with blushing emojis.

Thinking with his dick, Micah sent her five hundred dollars through an app on his phone. He fantasized about sharing his own virginity with Natalie. His imagination ran wild with visions of the future: cute dates, a beautiful wedding, a bestselling novel, a suburban house, a couple of kids, and maybe a dog or two. He saw the potential for true love with Natalie.

But she didn't show up at the diner.

And she didn't read his messages.

He put two and two together. He downloaded one of her images and performed a reverse image search on Google. He sighed as he scrolled through the results. The image was stolen from an Instagram model with over ten million followers. The account was verified, too. The model was visiting a 'friend' in Dubai.

"Catfished," Micah muttered. "No, *scammed*. Some guy, probably in another country. I should have known. I'm not getting my money back. No way. Goddammit..."

He rubbed his face with both hands and groaned in frustration. With one quick search, his dreams turned into nightmares. He envisioned a lonely future in a dingy studio apartment with a cat or bird, living off a diet comprised of noodles and tap water. He closed his MacBook and shoved his phone into his pocket. He gave up on 'Natalie.'

He beckoned to the red-haired waitress as she approached his booth. She carried a tray with two plates and two mugs. The name tag on her chest read: *Molly*.

He said, "Excuse me. Can I get the bill?"

"Oh, sure," Molly said. She lifted her order pad and flipped to Micah's bill. She said, "So... you only had the coffee?"

"Yeah."

Molly said, "Okay. That'll be four dollars and ninety-five cents." She tore his bill off the order pad and slapped it down on the table. She puckered her lips, then she said, "So you got stood up, huh?"

"Wha–What?" Micah stuttered, baffled by the personal question.

"Don't worry about it. It happens to everyone. I mean, really, some guy was stood up last week in this diner. Right over there, in that corner booth."

"Oh..."

"You're handling it better than that other guy. He actually started crying. You believe that? His eyes were like *sprinklers*. I had to scrub the table *and* the window. He was hysterical. Honestly, I thought I was going to have to call the police or... or an ambulance or something like that. I tried to help him out, but he wasn't hearing it."

"Oh," Micah repeated, a hint of discomfort in his voice.

Molly continued, "I don't judge, though. It's none of my business, but I try to be helpful when I see situations like that. I've been stood up before. Really, I've…"

Micah stopped listening. He figured she just loved the sound of her own voice—a real chatterbox. His attention drifted towards the waitress behind the counter.

Her name was Mackenzie McKee. Her long, curly black ponytail swung from side to side with the slightest movement of her head. She stood five-five, about six inches shorter than Micah. She had a shapely figure. She couldn't hide it under her bland uniform—a red polo shirt, black pants, work shoes. Her green eyes were flecked with gold. She emanated an aura of kindness.

Micah's eyes twinkled with hope. Butterflies swarmed in his stomach. His heart tap danced on his sternum. Behind the counter, in a local 24-hour diner, he found the most beautiful girl in the world. It was love at first sight. He couldn't take his eyes off her. Her smile made him smile, her laugh made him laugh.

He gasped as she looked in his direction. She caught him staring, but she didn't stop smiling. Like Molly and the other waitresses, she was always friendly while on the job.

Micah put his MacBook in his laptop bag and hopped up to his feet, interrupting Molly's endless rambling.

He threw a ten-dollar bill on the table and said, "Keep the change. Thank you."

"Okay, thank you, too. Have a nice day!"

Micah hurried out of the diner without looking back. He climbed into a black 2010 Toyota Prius in the parking lot.

As he reversed from the parking spot, he said, "Come on, Micah. What are you doing? Why are you always running?"

Chapter Three

Heights

Julian Lopez leaned over a balcony railing on the third floor of an indoor shopping mall. He watched the ground floor. The customers marched like ants, forming two lines moving in opposite directions. They chatted and laughed, they snapped selfies and shot short videos, and they shopped at the stores and kiosks. There were some bored faces in the crowd— little boys who didn't want to shop with their mothers—but the atmosphere was generally pleasant.

He turned his attention to the second floor. He saw a young, beautiful Hispanic woman—Gabriela Luna—standing outside of a Victoria's Secret with two other young ladies. They were waiting for a pair of friends. They chatted about the day and their lives, gossiping about old classmates and criticizing their workplaces. Their laughter occasionally echoed through the mall.

"Why couldn't you just say 'yes?' Am I *that* bad?" Julian whispered, sniffling. "Are you laughing at me? Did you tell 'em?"

Ten minutes earlier, while she was alone, Julian had approached Gabriela. They attended the same community college and shared an English class. He didn't expect to see her at the mall, he went out to try to socialize and escape from his dark hole of depression, but he seized the opportunity when he saw her alone. He had asked her on a date.

And she respectfully declined.

He replayed her words in his head until they sounded foreign: *'I'm sorry, but I have a boyfriend. Thanks for asking. I'm sorry, but tengo novio. I'm sorry, pero tengo novio. Lo siento, pero tengo novio.'* The funny thing was that Julian spoke Spanish, but he still couldn't understand Gabriela's rejection anymore.

Julian wiped the mucus from his nose and said, "I should have just stayed quiet. What was I thinking, man? I'm so fucking stupid."

He turned away and stared up at the ceiling. His eyes stung as he tried to stop himself from blinking. *Don't do it, don't do it, don't do it,* he told himself. He couldn't hold it. Rivers of tears rushed down his blushed cheeks as he blinked. He covered his eyes with his forearm. He took a piece of tissue out of his back pocket and wiped his face under his arm.

He thought about running out of the mall, but there was a storm brewing in his head. A whirlwind of emotions threw him for a loop. He felt sad, angry, embarrassed, and afraid. Gabriela's rejection was simple, quiet and gentle, but Julian felt insulted and humiliated. He believed she was talking about him with her friends—mocking him, *disrespecting him*.

Gritting his teeth and growling in anger, he gripped the rail and tugged on it. He pushed and pulled, pushed and pulled, and *pushed* and *pulled*, as if he were trying to break it. Suicide crossed his mind. He envisioned himself yelling Gabriela's name and then throwing himself over the balcony. He wondered if it would haunt her conscience for the rest of her life.

A six-year-old girl, Kiki Long, skipped up to the balcony. Mouth wide open, she pressed her face against the glass partition. She exhaled loudly, fogging up the glass. She could barely reach the railing above her. She sidestepped left and right while humming the melody of some pop song she had heard in her older sister's bedroom.

Gavin Long, her father, pushed a stroller to a set of sofas behind them. He sat down and shook a small stuffed teddy bear in front of his baby boy. His wife, Whitney, and his twelve-year-old daughter, Faith, shopped at an American Eagle Outfitters nearby. He saw Julian from the corner of his eye, but he didn't notice his agony. He saw a regular guy waiting for a friend or taking a break from work.

Loud but not quite shouting, he said, "Hey, hey, hey. Be careful over there, hun."

"*O*–kay," Kiki said without glancing back.

"I'm serious, baby. Stay away from the railing. Come sit with me. Play with your brother."

"*O*–kay," Kiki repeated with a hint of disappointment in her voice.

She stepped away from the balcony. She bounced on one foot, then she spun around like a figure skater while humming the same melody. She narrowly avoided a collision with Julian. She smiled at him—a big, toothless grin—then she danced around him.

Like her father, she wasn't intimidated by him. She giggled as she skipped across the bridge.

Julian gritted his teeth and tightened his grip on the railing as he watched her. Her gust of happiness fanned the flames of his rage. In Kiki, a *six*-year-old girl, he saw every female who ever rejected him. His mind was dominated by vulgar words: *little bitch, fucking slut, cheating whore, disgusting cunt*. He didn't know her name, he had never seen her before, but he knew he hated her.

Puffing and huffing, he walked away. He approached a Foot Locker store at the end of the bridge, then he took a right and followed the path. He was met by dozens of window-shoppers. A man bumped into him. A woman's large bag hit his stomach. Another man crashed into him. They kept walking as if nothing had happened—no apologies. He felt like he was walking against a stampede.

"No, no, no," he muttered as tears filled his eyes. "This isn't right. She's just going to grow up like the rest of them. Like Nicole, like Jessica, like Jackie, like Maribel, *like Gabriela...* Sluts... cunts..."

He turned around and walked back to the Foot Locker. He paced in front of the store while constantly glancing at Kiki on the bridge. He could see Gavin feeding his son with a nursing bottle. He spotted some shoppers walking on the parallel path, chattering and giggling.

Kiki took a Barbie doll out of her brother's stroller, then she raced back to the balcony. She stood on her tiptoes and tapped the doll's feet along the railing while humming. In her world of make-belief, she imagined the doll dancing on a tightrope while she watched from an audience of dazzled viewers.

Julian took a step towards the bridge, then he turned around and faced the Foot Locker. He hopped in place and frowned.

"Don't be a pussy, man," he whimpered. "Do it before Gabby leaves. She needs to see this. *Everyone* needs to see this. Man up. Be a fucking Alpha. Be a Chad."

He took a deep breath, then he marched back to the balcony. He wiped his face with his sleeve, then he leaned forward with his arms folded over the railing near Kiki. He stared up at the ceiling and tried to act natural. His mind was volcanic, erupting with bloody images of extreme violence. He grinned, then he frowned, and then he forced himself to smirk.

Kiki stopped beside him, doll on the railing. Mouth hanging open, she stared at him with a set of big, glimmering puppy eyes. Julian glanced at her, looked back up at the ceiling, glanced at her again, and then gazed down at the ground floor. He felt like he was avoiding eye contact with his crush—scared, confused, awkward.

Go ahead, he thought. *Call me a monster. Call me ugly. No, call me hideous. You know you want to, you little bitch.*

The girl said, "My name's Kiki."

Julian's lips trembled and head shuddered. He didn't expect her to talk to him. He kept his eyes on the customers below. He pictured himself dousing them with gasoline and setting them aflame, like a kid torching ants with a magnifying glass at a park. He heard their shrieking—*their begging*—in his head. The visions of mayhem calmed him.

Kiki held her doll up to him and said, "This is my best friend, Dee Dee. Not Kiki, *Dee Dee.* It's kinda the same, but not really. She loves to dance, just like me. But mommy says I'm prettier." She laughed as she stroked the doll's hair. Her eyes widened. She said, "Oh, look."

She unzipped her jacket pocket and took another toy out. It was a blue spherical fish with white eyes and orange puckered lips. She squeezed it, causing the eyes to expand and bulge.

She giggled, then she said, "Look what it can do!" She made her eyes as wide as possible. With unafraid enthusiasm, she said, "*Big eyes!* My daddy can do it bigger. You wanna meet my daddy, mister?"

Julian tilted his head and furrowed his brow. *Why aren't you running? Why aren't you screaming? Why aren't you vomiting?*—he thought. Suffering from rejection after rejection, his general opinion of females was poisoned. He expected her to run as soon as she saw his receding hairline, acne scars, and crooked nose.

The truth was: he attacked himself more than anyone else. He himself was his biggest critic and his worst bully. He saw a monster in the mirror when everyone else saw an average Joe. Self-consciousness had a way of warping the mind. He heard whispers from people without voices, and he felt like he was being stared at by a crowd of blind people.

Kiki was nice to him—*genuinely nice*—but he heard condescension in her soft voice. He hated her, and he only hated her because she was born a female.

"Are you okay?" Kiki asked before puckering her lips.

Julian spotted a cop and a security guard approaching the bridge. He glanced over his shoulder and made brief eye contact with Gavin. The man's eyes were dim with concern. Kiki's mother, Whitney, stood beside him with their oldest daughter. They had just finished shopping, carrying bags from several clothing stores.

Gavin yelled, "Kiki, baby, come here! Time to go!"

Julian grabbed Kiki under the armpits and hoisted her onto the railing. In an instant, the innocent wonder in Kiki's eyes was replaced with pure dread. She heard the panic in her father's voice. His fear amplified *her* fear. Parents lived vicariously through their children—and vice versa. Her eyes said something along the lines of: *please don't hurt me, mister.*

"Kiki!" Gavin shouted as he sprung up to his feet.

Whitney screamed, "No! What are you–"

Julian pushed Kiki off the balcony.

As she plummeted to the ground, she yelled, "Mo–"

One-point-seventy-five seconds.

It took Kiki one-point-seventy-five seconds—less than *two* measly seconds—to fall fifteen meters and hit the ground. It wasn't even enough time to finish yelling for her mommy. She hit the floor head-first at nearly forty miles per hour. The loud, dull, bone-crunching *thud* of her small body colliding with the floor echoed through the mall, followed by horrified shrieks, an opera of gasps, and a stampede of footsteps.

"Oh my God!" a woman shouted.

"Move, move, move," a young man said.

Another woman yelled, "Call 911!"

More shrieks.

More gasps.

Gavin rushed to the balcony. He leaned over the railing and looked down at the ground floor. *Kiki!*— his mouth was open, but he couldn't scream. He was struck with a sudden bout of dizziness. He felt like his organs were moving in his abdomen. Nausea twisted his intestines, forcing them to constrict over his stomach. His lungs were vacuumed by the shock and awe.

Kiki lay on her stomach, her left arm under her abdomen and the other bent behind her back like a boomerang. Skin and skull, her head was split open from her crown to her nose. Part of her brain was ejected from her skull. Blood gushed out in spurts, painting the floor with broad strokes. It was thick and slimy, as if it were mixed with a gelatinous substance, but it was all red—*deep red*. The blood pooled under her face and chest.

Her spine was broken from her neck to the small of her back. Her ribs, collarbones, arms, and shoulders didn't fare much better. A broken bone even stuck out of her elbow. The fall obliterated her, shattering nearly every bone across her upper body. She was dead before she knew it. Resuscitation was not an option. Yet, she still held Dee Dee, her Barbie doll, in her right hand. The toy fish floated in her blood, drifting away from her body.

A man rushed towards her to perform first-aid, unaware of the severity of her wounds—or perhaps hopelessly optimistic. The fish's eyes grew as he stepped on the toy.

'Big eyes!'

"No, God, no!" Whitney cried as she stumbled towards the balcony.

Gavin snapped out of his trance. His life changed in the blink of an eye—in two seconds. He was furious and heartbroken. He was scared and confused. He wanted to kill Julian while racing down to save Kiki. But he knew he had to protect Whitney, Faith, and his baby first. He was already haunted by images of Kiki's corpse. The image of her open skull was scarred into his retinas. He couldn't allow his family to suffer the same fate.

He turned and pushed Whitney back before she could reach the balcony. She kept pushing forward, but she couldn't overpower him. So, she slapped and clawed at his face while sobbing hysterically. Faith fell on the sofa, staring vacantly at the balcony in disbelief. She swayed in every direction, fading in and out of consciousness. She mouthed: *oh my God.* Her baby brother cried in the stroller, and his cries were laced with pain, as if he already knew about his sister's tragic death.

"No! No! No!" Whitney yelled. "My baby! Kiki! My baby!"

Gavin whispered into her ear, but his words were drowned out by the pandemonium at the shopping mall.

Julian stared at Kiki's corpse from above, stunned. *Her head popped,* he thought, *just like in Scanners.* The aftermath looked awful, the gore was atrocious, but it didn't look painful. It happened so fast. Death called out to him. At that moment, suicide didn't seem so bad. Tears of relief in his eyes, he grabbed the railing with both hands. He put one foot on the railing, then he pulled himself towards it. He was ready to fall and join Kiki in the afterlife.

"Gabriela! *Gabriela!*" he yelled. "Look at–"

Before he could throw himself over, the cop tackled him.

"No! Wait! Let me go! Let me go!" Julian shouted as he squirmed underneath the burly man.

The cop barked, "Stop resisting!"

"No! I'm sorry! Please let me go! Please!"

"Put your hands behind your back! *Now!*"

"No!"

The cop wrestled him until he took control of his arms. He rolled him onto his stomach and handcuffed him. He dug his knee into Julian's spine and pinned him to the floor. He called for a wagon and sent the security guard down to control the crowd and check on Kiki.

Julian wiggled underneath him. He heard the police chatter on the cop's radio and the Long family's anguished cries. He stared at his reflection on the glass, hot tears rolling across his nose and cheek. He only thought about hurling himself over the balcony. He sought a quick and painless death. He scratched the officer's pants, hoping to grab his pistol.

The cop squeezed the nape of Julian's neck and hissed, "Stop it, boy."

"Kill me," Julian squeaked out in a weak, pathetic voice.

The cop leaned to his right and examined the situation on the ground floor. He pressed the push-to-talk button on his radio and updated his dispatcher.

Julian repeated, "Kill me…"

Chapter Four

Introductions

Micah sat in the driver's seat of his car, parked in front of Mario's Diner. The dashboard clock read: *2:14 AM*. He had spent the last five days visiting the diner at different times of the day, hoping to catch Mackenzie during one of her shifts. To his disappointment, she didn't work the breakfast shift every morning, she avoided the lunch rush, and she wasn't around during dinner.

That night, through the storefront windows, he saw Mackenzie serving a trucker at a booth. She poured coffee into his mug with a tender smile on her face. And her smile was infectious. Alone in his car, Micah chuckled as he watched her prance from patron to patron. He admired her strength and determination. She worked a difficult job for minimum wage without complaining.

"Duh," Micah whispered. "Her shift was probably just ending the last time I saw her, so she must be working the graveyard shift every night. She's a night owl, like me. We're perfect for each other, aren't we?"

He adjusted the rear-view mirror and examined himself. Hair wax gave his curly locks a natural luster. He wore a black jacket over his nicest shirt—a gray, long-sleeve Polo Ralph Lauren shirt. He ironed his black jeans and cleaned his matching suede desert boots. He dressed himself using tips from fashion blogs and pictures of celebrities as a reference.

He stared at his reflection in the mirror and said, "Okay, Micah, don't fuck it up this time. It's easy, right? You talk a little about yourself, you ask questions about her, and you just... you stay confident. Confidence is key. You can do this. You *can* do this."

He grabbed his laptop bag and hopped out of his car. He took a deep breath, then he blew out a cloud of steam. He approached the diner. He walked through the puddles, water splashing with each step, but he felt like he was trudging through quicksand. The sidewalk stretched into endless slabs of concrete, pushing the diner away.

Micah's legs trembled under him. He leaned against a parking meter and took a second to regain his balance. His vision focused, and the sidewalk shrank to its regular size. He pulled his cell phone out of his pocket and laughed nervously, acting as if he had stopped to read a hilarious text message from a friend.

The door chime rang as he entered the diner.

"Hello," Mackenzie said as she approached the entrance. "Bar, table, or booth. It's a quiet night, so you got yourself lots of options."

Micah was caught off guard by her eyes— *emeralds*, beautiful emeralds. He thought about complimenting her, but his tongue was twisted into knots like his shoelaces.

"B–Booth," he croaked out.

Mackenzie nodded and said, "Sure thing. Please follow me."

Micah couldn't stop his eyes from wandering down to her ass. *Big, round… soft?*—he thought. He had never touched a woman's ass before. Her hips swung ever so slightly, hypnotizing him like a pendulum.

Mackenzie said, "Here we go. Best seat in the house."

"Thank you," Micah said.

He sat in a booth in the corner of the diner. He could see the four-lane road in front of the restaurant to his right, and the rest of the interior of the diner in front of him. The temperature was pleasant—not too cold, not too warm. All of the booths shared the same type of seating—wine vinyl upholstery—but his seat felt inexplicably comfortable.

He said, "Yeah, this is, um… This is cozy."

"Told ya," Mackenzie winked at him. She grabbed her order pad and a pen. She asked, "So, what can I get you started with?"

"Some coffee would be great."

"Great. Creamer and sugar's on the table to your right. Here's a menu if you'd like something to eat. I recommend the key lime pie. We have some platters, too. Anything else, just ask."

"Tha–Thank you."

"I'll be back with your coffee in a sec."

Micah glanced at her ass again. He tugged on his collar, then he swiped at his brow with the back of his hand. He didn't realize he was sweating. He took off his coat and checked his armpits. He sighed in relief. He didn't have any pit stains—*yet*. He dabbed his forehead, cheeks, and neck with a napkin while keeping an eye out for the waitress.

"Calm down," he told himself, his shaky voice barely above a whisper. "You're doing good so far. Just act natural. Do your thing, Micah."

He took his MacBook out of his bag and placed it on the table in front of him. He opened his web browser, then he opened his latest project on Microsoft Word. It was a manuscript titled: *Heretics*. He typed a few words, then he deleted them, and then he typed a couple more words. Like an author suffering from writer's block, he repeated the process over and over.

Except he wasn't trying to finish his work, he was just trying to *look* busy in front of Mackenzie to impress her.

Mackenzie approached the booth with a mug and a coffee pot. She filled the mug, then she asked, "Ready to order?"

"Um, yeah, I'll take the... Just a slice of the key lime pie, please."

"Ahh, I see you're a man of excellent taste," Mackenzie said.

"Yeah, well, um... It–It's your recommendation, right? So, you're, um... you're a woman of excellent taste."

"I guess I am," the waitress responded with a smirk. "I'll be right back with that pie. Give me another sec."

"Yeah, sure. Take your time."

Micah couldn't help but smile. He replayed their conversation in his head, criticizing himself while gushing over Mackenzie. He thought: *I need to be smoother. Stop stuttering, start smirking. Did we do some sexual innuendo? She smiled when she said she had good taste. Was she talking about her... pussy?* He blushed, then his cheeks inflated as he held in his laughter.

He watched as Mackenzie brought a platter of pancakes, scrambled eggs, sausage, bacon, and hash browns to a trucker at the bar. An elderly man at a booth in the opposite corner beckoned to her. She gave him half a curtsy as she approached his table. Micah couldn't hear their voices or read their lips, but he saw them smiling and chuckling. She brought an aura of happiness with her.

"She's a real angel," he whispered. "Everyone loves her... Everyone..."

He cocked his head back as the waitress looked his way. She held a finger up at him and mouthed: *'one more second!'*

Micah just nodded. He focused on his computer. *Don't look at her, don't make it obvious,* he told himself. He couldn't focus on his manuscript, so he read the news instead. He stumbled upon an article with a headline that read: *Six-year-old girl thrown from third-floor mall balcony.* It was a one-sentence horror story.

And it piqued his interest.

He skimmed through the article and read about Julian Lopez's despicable actions. The article recounted eyewitness accounts, described Kiki Long's grotesque injuries in graphic detail, and featured some quotes from the police. Julian's motives were still under investigation, although he was quoted as saying he was 'looking for someone to hurt' after being rejected by a woman at the mall.

The article's author also profiled Julian. He described Julian as a radical incel with alt-right views and a deep-seated hatred for women.

On Google, Micah searched: *"Kiki Long" pictures.*

He was relieved by the results. There were no clear pictures of Kiki's corpse on the internet. A video was uploaded by a shopper, but it only showed the chaos after the incident. He couldn't lie to himself, though. A part of him was disappointed. He wanted to see just how far he could go when it came to his exploration of death and the macabre.

He visited another forum for incels. He saw users mocking the mainstream media for blaming them as a whole for one person's actions. Some condemned Julian's actions while others praised him. Most of them posted cliché memes to troll the 'guests'— those viewing the forum without registering. The internet—anonymity—brought the worst out in people.

"Sorry about the wait," Mackenzie said as she approached him. She placed the plate on the table and said, "It's as fresh as it gets."

"Thank you very much. It looks delicious."

Ask her if she wants a bite, Micah told himself.

Mackenzie said, "My favorite." She put her hands in her pockets and asked, "So, what are you working on? Got a paper due or something?"

Micah nodded, then he shook his head. He said, "No, not a paper. Just, um… just reading the news and doing some research for work."

"We appreciate the company, but you came to a diner at 2 AM to read the news?"

The waitress giggled. Micah returned the laughter, although his laugh sounded unnatural. He leaned back and rubbed the nape of his neck. He was sweating again. *Stay cool, everything's fine,* he thought.

He said, "Actually, I've been having some trouble sleeping lately. Maybe it's the stress, maybe it's the loneliness. I'm single, you know?"

He bit his bottom lip and grunted to clear his throat. He was afraid he sounded desperate.

He continued, "Anyway, I've been craving some homecooked food. I'm not a great cook myself. And, um… the company's nice. I like this place. It's cozy."

"Yeah, I get ya," Mackenzie said. "But you won't find much company around here at this hour. You're better off going to a bar or even a McDonald's if you're looking for company. Nothing but truckers, drunk businessmen, and the elderly around here. You might bump into some drunk frat boys if it's a game night, but that's only if they get kicked out of iHop or Denny's."

"Oh, really? Wow, it sounds kind of... tough. Do those, um... 'drunks' ever bother you?"

"Bother me?"

"Yeah, you know, like... like all that stuff on the news and Twitter. Catcalling, touching, sexual harassment."

"*Oh,*" Mackenzie said with a raised brow. "No, no, I've never experienced anything like that. One of my friends, she got spanked by some douchebag once. The guy got kicked out and banned for life."

With disappointment in his voice, Micah said, "A slap on the wrist."

"Exactly. I'm lucky it hasn't happened to me. I've had to clean vomit and even piss in the past, but no one's ever harassed me or attacked me or anything like that."

From the other end of the diner, the elderly man yelled, "Excuse me, miss! Excuse me!"

Mackenzie said, "Sorry, gotta get back to it. Enjoy your meal."

Micah leaned forward and said, "Wait. My name's Micah. What's yours?"

Mackenzie turned around, walked backwards, and pointed at the nametag clinging to her chest. She said, "Mackenzie." She spun around and, as she walked away, she said, "Anything else, just ask."

"Mackenzie," Micah repeated under his breath. "It's beautiful."

He watched her, eyes shining with wonder and love. He felt like he was watching an endangered species—a unique, beautiful animal. He chuckled as he heard her giggle. He didn't know why she was laughing, but her happiness made him happy. He felt a jolt of jealousy as the elderly man patted her forearm. The man apologized for asking too many questions while thanking her for her patience.

As she walked away from the booth, Mackenzie caught Micah staring at her. She waved at him as she strolled back to the counter. Micah's heart fluttered around in his chest, like a bird in a cage, while doubt flooded the sulci of his brain, like rain flooding the canals in Venice. He was happy because she waved at him, and sad because she didn't return to his booth.

He ate his pie, sipped his coffee, and browsed the internet. He researched satanism and satanic rituals, cults and their leaders, and traditional religion for his latest manuscript. Yet, he couldn't stop thinking about Mackenzie. He thought about using her name for a character in his book. He even considered changing the genre from horror to romance for her.

"I can write our love story," he whispered. "Then maybe it'll come true."

The door chime rang as the elderly man exited the diner. A trucker sat at the bar, eating his meal while flicking his greasy thumb across his cell phone's screen. A man in a suit sat at another booth, carving away at a stack of pancakes while reading spreadsheets with graphs on his laptop. The diner was calm and quiet. The guests could take care of themselves.

Micah's mind wandered to another subject: *incels*. He visited the forum again and browsed the threads.

He studied the users, trying to understand their experiences, their rationales, and their intentions. The men felt entitled to sex with women. A history of rejection, a bevy of insecurities, and years of loneliness left them disillusioned and angry.

And, unable to bottle it within, their self-hatred turned outward. They blamed women, handsome men, the media, and contemporary culture. They lashed out at society—sometimes violently.

Micah saw a reflection of himself in some of those anonymous users. He was a virgin, he was lonely, and he was insecure. He had never kissed a girl before, either. He was rejected by every girl he approached. But he didn't hate women. He envied handsome men and happy couples, but he didn't despise them.

A spark of hope still flickered in his heart. He wasn't ready to end his pursuit of happiness. He believed there was someone out there for him—for everyone.

Mackenzie asked, "Need more coffee?"

Micah closed the tab on his web browser. Captivated by the disturbing posts, he didn't notice her approach his booth.

He said, "Yeah, sure."

"How was the pie?" Mackenzie asked as she filled his mug.

"It was, um… delicious. Not too sweet, not too tart. Thank you."

"No problem. Glad you enjoyed it."

Mackenzie sat down across from him, crossed her legs, and groaned in exhaustion. Micah's eyes squinted to slits and his mouth fell open.

Mackenzie giggled, then she said, "Oh, that was rude of me. I should have asked first. I just thought it'd be okay since you said you wanted company. I can leave you alone if you–"

"No, no!" Micah interrupted. "Um, I mean... you can stay. It's fine. Well, your boss isn't going to get mad, is he? I don't want you to get fired or anything like that."

"Ahh, don't worry about him. It's a slow night. And it's time for my break anyway."

"Cool, cool."

'Cool, cool?' Micah thought. *Do people still say 'cool?' Maybe I should have said 'lit?' Too late. Maybe next time. I'm doing good right now. She's sitting there because she likes me. She thinks I'm interesting. Maybe she thinks I'm cute, too. Holy shit, I'm making progress. Stay cool. No, no. Stay 'lit,' Micah.*

Mackenzie chose to spend her break with Micah because he didn't seem as busy as the businessman and he looked friendlier than the trucker. She wasn't physically attracted to him, but she wasn't repulsed by his appearance, either. The truth was: she was bored and lonely, and she wanted to do something nice for Micah.

Micah said, "So, um... uh..." He looked at the nametag on her chest. He said, "Mackenzie McKee. That's a pretty name."

Mackenzie snickered, then she said, "Thanks. Micah's pretty cool. You got a last name, Micah?"

"Yeah."

Ten seconds of silence passed.

Mackenzie huffed and grinned, then she said, "*Well?*"

"Oh, yeah, my last name is Watson. Micah Watson."

"It's nice to meet you, Mr. Watson."

The waitress reached out for a handshake. Micah wiped his clammy palm on his knee, then he shook her hand. He memorized the grooves across her fingers and palm. Her hand was smaller than his, like a child's hand. He was amazed by her soft, warm skin. He felt like he was holding hands with a lover. He released her hand after seven seconds—the best seven seconds of his life.

He dropped his hands under the table. He rubbed his sweaty palms on his thighs while trying to keep his composure.

He said, "It's nice to meet you, too, Ms. McKee. So, um... we were talking about something, right? About your customers?"

"Oh yeah. Truckers, businessmen, frat boys... lonely fellas and ladies... insomniacs. We see a little bit of everything here. The rowdy drunks are the worse. They make the job harder—more cleaning and stuff—but like I said, they've never hurt me. I like this job. I don't want to stay forever, but... it's not as bad as it looks. So, what do you do, Micah?"

"I work at Carlotta's. I don't make the pizza. I just deliver it."

"Oh, so you're a 'comrade,' hmm?"

"A comrade?" Micah repeated.

"Yeah, a fellow pink-collar worker. So, you know what it's like serving customers. Some are great, some are awful, right? I bet you've got some crazy stories."

Micah shrugged and shook his head—*nope*. Mackenzie puckered her lips and returned the shrug. The silence returned, every second lingering longer than the last. Micah didn't want to lose her interest. Although she worked as a waitress, he knew he couldn't impress her with a job title like 'pizza delivery driver.'

He said, "You know, I also write books. I'm not like Stephen King or Dean Koontz or Tom Clancy or... I'm not a big author, you know? But it makes me some extra money on the side and it's a fun job, too. I really like it."

"Wow," Mackenzie responded, wide-eyed. "Why didn't you tell me I was serving a famous author?"

"No, I'm not fame–"

"So, what kind of books do you write?"

Mackenzie leaned forward in her seat, elbows on the table and eyes sparkling with curiosity. Micah smiled and took a sip of his coffee. He thought about the perfect response, obsessing over every detail.

He grunted, then he said, "Well... I–I dabble in this and that. Horror, fantasy, um... LitRPGs, you know? Those are like, um... like books with elements from video games. I don't write a lot of those, but, um... I mostly write thrillers. Yeah, I'm more of a thriller guy."

"Wow, impressive. I love a good thriller. Anything I've read?"

"O–Of mine?"

"Of course."

"I don't... No, I don't think so. I'm small fry."

Hmm—the sound escaped Mackenzie's sealed lips as she leaned back in her seat, hands tucked into the pockets of her waist apron. She looked out the window, watching as cars zoomed past the diner.

She said, "I've always wanted to be a writer or a painter or a musician... A creator, you know?" She looked Micah in the eye and said, "I have an idea for this book. I think it's an amazing idea, but I just can't get it down on paper. It's too complicated and 'unique.' So, there's this guy, right? And, one day, he finds out he has a superpower. He tries to hide it at first, but then a bad guy shows up and starts threatening his friends and family. So, he has to..."

Mackenzie's steady face broke into a smile. She laughed and slapped her knee. Micah laughed with her, although he didn't catch the joke.

The waitress said, "I'm sorry, I'm sorry. I'm just kidding. I wish I could work as a creator, I love painting and sculpting with clay, but I don't have any ideas for any books. I'm no storyteller. I just know you writers hate it when people try to tell you their ideas. You must get that a lot, huh? 'Hey, I have this great idea for a book, what can I do with it? How can I make a million dollars with it?' But it must be exciting to get your work out there—to express yourself. That's great, Micah. I'm happy for you."

Micah's eyelids and nose twitched. He was overwhelmed with joy. *She's happy for me, she cares about me, she loves me,* he thought. He liked her sense of humor and he appreciated her kindness. In his eyes, she was the spitting image of perfection—the embodiment of beauty. He turned in his seat and looked out the window. He saw his tight-lipped smile in the reflection. Tears of joy pooled in his eyes and clung to his eyelashes. A single blink would have led to a cascade of tears.

"Are you okay?" Mackenzie asked. "I'm sorry if I offended you or if I brought up any bad memories. I was–"

"No, no," Micah interrupted as he looked at her. "I'm a… I was just… I'm happy that I met you. You're a good person, Mackenzie."

"Aww, that's sweet. You're a good person, too, Micah. Someday, I'll have to ask you for your autograph. Then, when you're big and famous, I can say I was one of your first fans."

"Really? Well, I can get you a copy of one of my books. I can get you copies of all of them. I've never done it before, but I'd be happy to autograph them for you."

Mackenzie shook her head and said, "No, I couldn't accept it."

"Why not?" Micah asked. "It's a gift. It's fine, really."

"I don't want to be a bother and... I just don't want any gifts right now."

The smile was wiped off Micah's face. He lowered his head in shame. Staring at his black coffee, a void of darkness in his mug, he thought: *she doesn't like me, she hates me, I'm a loser*. He saw the world in black and white. It was either this or that, nothing in between. So, she either loved him or hated him. He was either perfect for her or he was a filthy, disgusting animal.

Looking to change the subject, Mackenzie asked, "Have you ever thought about quitting your job at Carlotta's?"

"Wh–Why?" Micah stuttered.

"To write. You can write more if you're not delivering pizza, right? And when you're not writing, when you need extra cash, you can drive for Uber. That's true independence, isn't it? God, what I would do to be my own boss..."

Micah wasn't a bestselling author. His book sales supplemented his income, but he wasn't rich by any means. Mackenzie's support and belief in him bolstered his confidence.

Her elbows on the table and her chin on her palms, Mackenzie asked, "Got any music on that thing?"

Micah said, "Umm, not really. I can go on YouTube if you want. What do you like to listen to?"

"Hmm... Don't laugh, okay? But I love—love, love, *love*—listening to nineties boy bands."

"Seriously?" Micah smirked.

"*Seriously*. It's nostalgic, you know? I grew up listening to a lot of that music. My older sister introduced me to *so* many bands. New Kids on the Block, NSYNC, the Backstreet Boys, O-Town, B2K... I just can't give it up. And Justin Timberlake. What a heartthrob, huh? The ramen noodle hair with the frosted tips, *wow*."

Mackenzie was joking about Justin Timberlake, but Micah didn't realize it. He looked at his reflection. He could see himself pulling off the singer's look.

He said, "My hair is–"

The door chime rang through the diner.

Mackenzie said, "Oh, sounds like break time's over."

As she hopped up to her feet, Micah asked, "Can we talk again later? Maybe tomorrow or the day after if you're free?"

The waitress responded, "Sure thing. If we're ever in the same place at the same time, let's do this again. Good luck with your book, friend." She winked at him and said, "Thanks for the chat, Micah."

"Tha–Thank you, too."

Micah placed his hand over his heart, as if he were about to say the Pledge of Allegiance. He dabbed the tears from his eyes with a napkin and chuckled inwardly. To him, their conversation was a date—*his first*. And, although she didn't commit to anything, he believed Mackenzie had agreed to meet him again. He told himself that he had sealed the deal for a second date. He saw an opportunity to win her heart, and he was determined to take it by any means necessary.

Chapter Five

The Wheels on the Bus

Steven West sat in the driver's seat of a yellow school bus. He parked behind an elementary school in a suburban neighborhood. A short bus parked behind him. High school students lined up in the alley beside the school. They chatted amongst themselves, tinkered with their cell phones, and snapped selfies while waiting for the bus. Some of them huddled behind a dumpster, taking tokes of marijuana from a glass pipe.

Steven glanced at his reflection on the rear-view mirror. There was a look of resentment in his dim, hateful eyes. He tugged on the handle beside his seat to open the door.

The chitter-chatter in the alleyway burst into the bus. He heard a little bit of everything from the teenagers. They spoke about sports, movies, celebrities, and other classmates. He heard a couple of swear words and even a few racial slurs, too. A girl shrieked, then her shrill laughter echoed through the neighborhood as one of the boys tickled her ribs and prodded her breasts. They were teenagers being teenagers.

Happiness wasn't always contagious, though. One person's happiness could aggravate another's depression.

The teenagers entered the bus, flashing their student ID cards at Steven as they walked past him. Steven looked out the windshield while occasionally glancing at them. He was supposed to check each ID card for security purposes—after all, he wasn't supposed to be driving strangers to the school in his bus—but he loathed those kids. He couldn't stand to look at them for more than a few seconds and their voices were like the incessant *buzz* of a fly to his ears.

He sighed upon spotting two teenagers in the alley—Guillermo Hernandez and Jessica Garcia. The line shrunk, but they weren't in a hurry to enter the bus and head to school. Instead, they leaned on the fence and kissed. Jessica squeezed Guillermo's shirt at the chest while Guillermo stuffed his hands into the back pockets of Jessica's jeans. They giggled, they whispered sweet talk into each other's ears, and they even moaned.

Steven honked, then he leaned to his right and yelled, "If you two want a ride to school, you better get in here now! I'm telling you: we don't got all day!"

The couple ignored him. They shared another big, sloppy kiss. Guillermo bit Jessica's bottom lip and pulled it away from her. Then they snickered. Steven tightened his grip on the steering wheel. Their happiness worsened his depression, their love amplified his anger. He felt disrespected by their behavior. *You're not the Alpha, you're just a kid,* he thought as he gritted his teeth. He honked the horn again, and he held it for three seconds.

He shouted, "If you don't get your butts in here, I'm going to report you as truant to the principal! I know that's you, Guillermo! You…"

'You little bastard!'—he stopped himself from insulting the student. He clenched his jaw and growled, struggling to control his anger. Guillermo scoffed at him. Jessica snickered, then she rolled her eyes. They grabbed their bags and headed to the bus.

As he flashed his ID at him, Guillermo asked, "Why you gotta act like such a dick all the time?"

"What'd you say to me?" Steven said in disbelief.

"You heard me, man."

"I heard you, but I wanted to give you a chance to pretend you *didn't* just say that."

"Whatever, man. I'm not scared of you. You're just the bus driver."

"Hey, show some respect, kid."

As he walked down the aisle between the seats, Guillermo said, "Oh yeah, you're the janitor, too. Congratulations, man. You're a real big fuckin' deal."

Steven glanced over his shoulder and sneered at him. He didn't check Jessica's ID. She showed it to him anyway, then she followed Guillermo. Steven's eyes widened as she entered his field of view. He couldn't stop himself from leering at her ass. He was aroused by her curvy figure. She was half his age—sixteen years old—but he was tempted by her. He swallowed the lump in his throat and shook his head, then he turned around before anyone could catch him ogling a teenager.

He drove away. The short bus followed his lead. They headed to the high school at the other side of town.

Steven's eyes wandered to the rear-view mirror, but he didn't care about the roughhousing or the ruckus. He kept his eyes on Guillermo and Jessica. The couple sat at the back of the bus beside the emergency exit. They kissed and fondled each other. Guillermo slipped his hand under the low-cut neckline of Jessica's shirt. He squeezed her breast under her bra. Jessica blushed. She liked it, but it was also embarrassing for her. She didn't know how to tell him to stop.

Steven sped up and slowed down inconsistently while swerving. Intoxicated by a cocktail of anger and arousal, he drove like a drunk driver. His fists were clenched around the steering wheel while his erect penis rubbed against his pants.

A female student yelled, "Oh my God! Slow down!"

Another girl asked, "Is he drunk or something?"

"He's in a hurry to mop the floors!" a teenage boy shouted.

Some of the students began booing, others laughed while mocking him, and the rest focused on their phones, their friends, and their homework. Guillermo and Jessica wrestled with their tongues. They didn't spare a second thought for their bus driver.

Yet, Steven couldn't stop thinking about them. He wanted Jessica all for himself. He wished he could kiss her, grope her, and *fuck her*. He tried to convince himself that sixteen wasn't too young. He knew it was irrational and immoral, but he was jealous of Guillermo.

"Goddamn you," he muttered as he watched the couple. "You just got lucky. She doesn't know any better. You little bastard…"

He caught a glimpse of his own reflection. He was an average guy, but he saw a monster in the mirror. He saw glowing zits, bushy eyebrows, a long nose, and dry, cracked lips. He cut his hair down to a buzz cut every week by himself. His stubble was patchy, bald spots across his jaw. He wore a baseball cap and loose clothes to try to hide himself from the world.

Guillermo, on the other hand, shined like a star. He played football for the varsity team, so he was athletic. His jawline was sharp and his cheekbones were high and protuberant. His face was smooth and hairless. He had a few pimples, but to Steven, they looked good on Guillermo. He saw them as accessories on his face.

He looked out the windshield again. He drove on a wide six-lane road. To the left, there were fields of strawberries. To the right, there was a grocery store, a couple of small shops, and a few houses.

He whispered, "You're a Chad, huh? You think you're better than me, don't you? Yeah, you do. And you think your dick is bigger than mine? You can please a girl and I can't, right? I'm nothing but a cuck to you… to everyone." His eyes watered and his face twisted in pain. He said, "God, I hate you all so much."

He sped through a red light. A pickup truck had to swerve to avoid a deadly collision. The driver, along with others behind him, honked at the bus.

"Holy shit, bro!" a teenager yelled.

The students looked out the windows. Their ridicule and laughter turned into panic and whimpering. Two of them tried to walk down the aisle between the seats, but they fell when Steven swerved again. Guillermo and Jessica stopped kissing. Their faces, creased in confusion, said something along the lines of: *what the hell is going on?*

They looked out the back window. The short bus was stuck at the red light behind them. It shrunk to a speck on the glass within seconds.

"Hey, what the fuck, man?!" Guillermo yelled.

"I'm scared," a girl cried.

A young man shouted, "Stop the bus!"

Steven put the pedal to the metal and roared, "You deserve this! You little bastards! Flaunting your tits and asses in my face! Talking shit every *fucking* day! Treating me like trash! Well, fuck all of you! Fuck you!"

He jerked the steering wheel to the left. The bus jounced over the median strip. It bounced like a low rider onto the oncoming lanes. Before he could drive it into the fields, he lost control of the vehicle. It tipped over and fell on its right side. The windshield cracked, the door flew open, and the windows shattered. The students fell on top of each other.

A horn ripped through the area, accompanied by the sound of screeching wheels. A sedan swerved onto the side of the road and rolled into the fields. The large, cherry-red pickup truck in the center lane was too close to stop. It pierced the bus through the ceiling, barreled over the students, and exited through the floor of the vehicle. It tore the bus in half. The wheels on the bus soared in every direction. The sound of the crash echoed through the city, like a bomb in Syria.

The bumper of the pickup truck was peeled off. The engine was crushed and set aflame, puffing out black clouds of smoke. The two front tires were flat. The windshield burst and the ceiling collapsed into the cab. The glass and the metal pierced the airbags, popping them within seconds of the collision.

A large shard of glass stabbed the driver's neck while the metal from the ceiling partially scalped him from behind, pushing his scalp forward and forcing his forehead to crease over. His left wrist was broken and his right arm was snapped at the elbow, the bone sticking out of the open fracture. He couldn't scream because he was choking on his own blood.

He could barely see due to the glass in his eyes. He saw a blur of red—every tint of the color of death. He heard crackling fire, clunking metal, and anguished shrieks. He felt like he was driving a hearse into hell. He reached for the door, but it was jammed. Gurgling sounds escaped his mouth, along with strings of gooey blood, as he tried to cry and scream. He reached for his seat belt, but he couldn't unbuckle it.

The truck kept rolling, leaving a trail of smoke and fire behind it.

Steven awoke three minutes after the crash. He was still strapped to his seat thanks to the seat belt. Glass shards sliced his cheeks and forehead. Blood leaked out of his nose and gums. His shoulder was busted, his ankle was twisted, and his ribs were cracked. A burning pain shot through his chest with each breath. He could only see in front of himself, although he heard the weeping behind him.

Mexican farmers watched the accident from the fields in aghast. Some of them held phones up to their ears and reported the accident. One farmer recorded the incident from his phone.

Steven unbuckled his seat belt. He screamed as he fell to the broken door. The landing amplified the pain in his shoulder and chest. He struggled to his feet. There was a fire between the two halves of the bus. Some seats and the undercarriage were set aflame by the crash. There were six bodies burning on the road between the two halves of the bus.

Only two of them were fully intact. The others were dismembered by the collision, a street littered with arms, legs, hands, and feet. One of the teenagers was decapitated. His burning head flew thirty meters away from the crash site. The bodies were burnt to a crisp, black flakes of their skin dancing with the breeze and flying through the air like cherry blossoms. Bright embers, homework, and sheets torn out of textbooks joined the charred skin in the air.

The students escaped through the emergency exit hatch on the ceiling at the front of the bus. A few climbed out through the broken windows above them, eager to escape the death trap that once took them to school every morning. A few students lay on piles of broken glass beside their seats, incapacitated. And some of those students were dead or dying. They cried out to their parents, desperate for rescue as the heat from the fire crawled towards them.

'Mom! Dad!'

'Help!'

'Mom!'

'Mommy!'

'Oh my God!'

'Somebody help!'

Steven followed a young teenager through the emergency exit. He hit the ground again, but he landed on his other shoulder. Yet, he still felt the stinging pain in his ribs.

"Goddammit," he cried while spraying saliva through his gritted teeth. "Fuck... Oh my... God... Ow..."

He staggered away from the bus and limped around the fire. He smiled as he spotted a group of students carrying Guillermo's body out of the bus through the other emergency exit on the ceiling. (The door in the back was jammed.) But Steven wasn't happy to see their cooperation. He was happy because Guillermo was fatally injured.

A large shard of glass had penetrated the side of Guillermo's head above his right ear. It cut halfway *into* his skull. It pierced his eye, flooding his eye socket with gelatinous blood, and stopped at his glabella—the space between his eyebrows. The entire right side of his face was drenched in blood. His left eye was wide open, cold and vacant. A piece of his brain oozed out of the cut on the side of his head, sliding across the glass towards the back of his head.

Jessica survived with some scratches, bruises, and cracked bones. She knelt beside Guillermo, grabbed the chest of his shirt, and shook him.

"Help him!" she cried out. "Please!"

The students didn't know what to do. It was a bloodbath unlike anything they had ever seen before. Two uninjured students stood on the median strip. The young man called his mother while the young woman streamed the aftermath of the crash on her cell phone via Instagram. She was scared, but something inside of her told her to record everything.

Steven lost his footing and fell to the ground. He groaned and whined as he stared up at the black smoke in the sky. Emergency sirens surrounded the crash from every angle, growing louder with each passing second. He sat up and stared at his feet. He had tripped on a student's severed arm. It was sooty and bloody, black and red. He couldn't tell if it belonged to a male or female student. He rose to his feet, bouncing on his only good foot.

He snickered, then he chuckled, then he laughed maniacally as he watched Guillermo's dead body. He was overjoyed by the mayhem. An ambulance stopped behind him. The paramedics hesitated for a moment after seeing the extent of the accident, then they bolted into action. Two police cruisers arrived in the oncoming lanes. Fire trucks from across the city were racing towards the crash, too.

From the median strip, the female student pointed at Steven and shouted, "It was him! *Him!* He–He did it on purpose! He drove... He drove..." She couldn't finish the sentence without her voice cracking. She cried, "Oh my God, please help my friends! That guy's crazy! He's fucking crazy!"

Steven limped away. He started crying and laughing at the same time. Fear and joy fought to express themselves through his bloody face. *The fields, the fields, the... fields,* he thought. The police called out to him, but he just shook his head, like a child walking away from his parents after an argument. He slipped on a burnt backpack and hit the pavement face-first before he could escape.

He was knocked unconscious. Although he was accused of causing a deadly accident, the cops rushed to help him, too.

Chapter Six

The Big Question

Micah sneered in disgust at his computer monitor. He watched the footage of the tragic bus accident. In the video, the sky was swallowed by black smoke, severed limbs were strewn across the bloodstained street, teenagers screamed and wept, and emergency sirens echoed through the street. It looked apocalyptic—*the end of the world*. The police pleaded with the public to stop circulating images and videos from the incident, but their efforts were fruitless. The footage flooded every social media website, shared and shared again like the latest dance craze.

Micah found the video on another incel forum: *www.fuck-less.com*. Steven West, the bus driver, wasn't a self-professed involuntary celibate. He didn't mingle with the incel community. His admission of guilt, however, caused the media to paint him as one of them. After the crash, in a state of hysteria, he admitted to purposely driving the bus into oncoming traffic because he was jealous of one of the students. And the incel community was happy to have him.

'AspiringAddict,' a member of the forum, wrote: *holy shit!! This dude's a fucking hero! He wiped out a couple of Chads and Stacys, and he still made it out alive!*

'BrainDeadCel' wrote: *Steven was the victim, but the media is saying he's a sick killer, like the rest of 'us.' He's not sick, he's a champion for our cause. He's a voice for the voiceless. Fucking idiots...*

Micah played another video. The footage depicted the driver in the pickup truck burning to death as he struggled to remove his belt and open the door. Some other drivers and pedestrians tried to help him, but the fire scared them away whenever they got close. The driver in the pickup truck unleashed a bloodcurdling shriek. Then it sounded like he was trying to say a name—perhaps his wife's or a child's. One of the pedestrians stuck his fingers into his hair and walked in circles.

The camerawoman kept repeating the same phrase under her breath: "Oh my God, oh my God, oh my God."

"Jesus Christ," Micah said.

He stopped the video and sat in silence for a minute. He was disgusted by the footage, but he thought about searching for more clips of accidents and murders. He questioned himself for a moment: *who am I? What's wrong with me?* He glanced around, as if he didn't recognize his own bedroom. It was a small and clean room.

There was a twin-sized bed in one corner, a desk with a computer in another, and a short bookcase in the other. The bookcase was full of true crime and horror novels.

He dressed himself in his finest clothes: a baby blue button-up shirt, a pair of dark blue jeans, and his favorite desert boots. He didn't own a mirror, so he used the front facing camera on his cell phone to style his hair. He tried to straighten his hair a bit with goops of gel. Then he grabbed a gift bag from his closet. He wiped the sweat, as well as some gel, from his forehead with the back of his hand.

He whispered, "This is it. I'm ready for her."

In the hall outside of his room, he ran into his mother, Anne Watson. She was fifty-one years old, but she was still glowing with youth. She carried a lightweight vacuum cleaner down the hall.

She said, "Oh, hey, honey. I haven't seen you in a couple of days. Did they change your schedule at that pizza place?"

Micah never explained to his parents that he had been visiting Mario's Diner at random times of the day for the past two weeks to meet Mackenzie. He knew it was strange. It was the behavior of a stalker. He didn't want to worry or upset them.

He said, "Um, yeah. I've just been busy."

"Well, they should really give you a more stable schedule, don't ya think? You're dependable, but that doesn't mean they can just take advantage of you whenever they want."

"Y–Yeah."

He tried to squeeze past her.

Anne smiled and asked, "And where are you off to now dressed so dapper?"

"Just, um… I'm going to meet a friend."

"*Oh,*" Anne said, eyes narrowed deviously. "A *girl*-friend?"

Micah's cheeks blushed while his eyelids and nose twitched. He was never comfortable talking to his parents about his love life.

He stuttered, "I–I'm... I–I..."

Anne adjusted the collar of his shirt and said, "Well, I'm glad you're getting yourself out there, honey. We were getting a little worried about you. A girlfriend will do you good. Now I'm not saying you have to marry someone and settle down, but... it's good to find someone to care about and to care about you. And you need the experience anyway, don't you? Didn't you watch that movie with me and your dad? What was it called... With that guy from The Office..."

Micah looked at the floor. He thought: *ah, shit. She's going to remember. She's going to say it again. I'm not even thirty yet.*

Wide-eyed, Anne said, "Oh! The 40-Year-Old Virgin!"

And there it is, Micah told himself.

Anne continued, "It's a funny, *funny* movie with a great message, right? But you don't want it to get to that point, Micah. You're young. You should be meeting people and experiencing love. There'll be some heartbreak, but it's worth it. Trust me, honey, it's an amazing part of life. It beats being stuck in your room all day. Anyway, if you need any help or advice or anything like that, you can always talk to me or your father. We're here for you, baby."

"Thanks," Micah said. He stepped past her and said, "I have to go now or I'll be late."

Anne said, "Oh, okay. Well, good luck! I love you!"

"Love you, too!"

He hurried out of the house before he could run into his father.

***

Micah sat at the bar, fidgeting on the stool. In front of him, he saw the cooks preparing burgers, steaks, chicken tenders, and French fries in the bustling kitchen. The waiting staff moved from patron to patron, ensuring the customers were satisfied with their meals. The diner was filled with families, couples, groups of friends, and a couple of individual patrons, their voices overlapping to create a discordant orchestra of gibberish.

Beverly 'Bev' Bennett approached Micah. Her sandy hair was tied in a bun. Tattoos decorated her knuckles. They appeared to be the heads of several animated characters. Micah only recognized the Hello Kitty head on her middle finger's knuckle. He thought it was cute.

Bev asked, "You ready to order?"

"Yeah, uh... No, actually, I'm not ready."

"Okay, no problem. I'll give you a couple more minutes with the menu, then I'll–"

"I'm sorry. It's not that I'm not ready to order, it's just that... Can I speak to Mackenzie? Mackenzie McKee? I saw her when I got here, but she just sort of disappeared. Is she available?"

"Oh, are you a friend of hers?"

"Well, yeah. *Yeah,* we're friends. We've been, you know, 'kicking it' for a couple of days."

"Kicking it?" Bev repeated as she snickered.

Micah shrugged and forced an awkward, toothy smile onto his face. He laughed with her, acting as if he were joking. *Why the hell did I say that?*–he thought.

Bev said, "I think Mackenzie's in the back talking to our *jefe*. She might come out again for thirty minutes, maybe a little more, but I think her shift is almost over. So, even if she starts serving you, you're going to end up with me. And, if you want to be a good customer, you'll have to tip double for the both of us. You're probably just better off with lil' ol' me, don't you think?"

"Oh, um… I don't care about tips."

"Well, we do. We kinda depend on 'em, you know?"

"That's not what I meant. I mean… I'll tip double, triple, quadruple… fifteen, twenty, twenty-five percent… Tipping isn't an issue for me. I just really need to see Mackenzie."

Bev puckered her lips, then she asked, "Why?"

Micah stuttered, "I–I have to ask her something."

The waitress bit her bottom lip as she examined Micah. The young man looked awkward, uncomfortable in his outfit and his own skin, but he seemed harmless.

She asked, "You're not a stalker, are you?"

Micah shook his head and stuttered, "N–No, of course not."

"Well… okay, what's your name?"

"Micah Watson."

"I'll let her know you're here. But, if she even *looks* scared when I mention your name, I'm kicking you out myself."

"Yeah, o–okay."

Micah sighed in relief. He tugged on his collar, then he checked his armpits. Sweat started to ooze through his shirt. He dabbed his neck and forehead with a napkin, then he took a sip of his water. He stared down at the bar, eyes darting left and right as he considered his options.

"Oh, hey, Mackenzie, funny seeing you here," he mumbled to himself. "No, no, it's too cliché. 'Hey, Mac…' Wait, I can, uh… 'Hey, Big Mac, how's your day going?' No, that's stupid. Girls don't want to be called 'Big Mac.' Just call her by her name. 'Hello, Mackenzie, how are you today?' Too formal? Yeah, too formal. I should…"

He glanced to his left. An elderly man sat on the stool beside him, nibbling on a slice of toast as he watched him. Micah smiled nervously and nodded at him. *Now's not the time to practice,* he thought, *just go with what you know.* He looked to his right and watched as Bev served the other customers. She wasn't in a hurry to deliver Micah's message.

Micah was afraid he'd drown in his sweat if Mackenzie didn't show up soon. He used another napkin to dry himself—and then another. Two minutes passed, but it felt like two hours, three minutes felt like three days, four minutes like four weeks. Doubt told him that he was going to be stood up by Mackenzie. Fear told him to run out of the diner before embarrassment stripped away his last shreds of confidence.

"She's coming, she's coming," he whispered, his eyes on his reflection on the metal napkin holder.

***

"Hey, Micah."

Micah closed his eyes upon hearing that feminine voice—Mackenzie's voice. A tender smile stretched across his face. His skin felt cool and dry, as if his sweat had crawled back into his pores. His heartbeat slowed. The storm in his mind dissipated. He felt like a newborn baby boy listening to his mother's lullaby.

Mackenzie sat on the other stool beside him. She asked, "What's up? What are you doing here? Bev told me you had to ask me something. It sounded urgent." She smirked and said, "She didn't want me to come out here, though. She said you looked a little, uh... How do I put this lightly? Like a serial killer in the making. Her words, not mine, okay?"

She giggled. Micah laughed with her. *She's teasing me,* he thought, *that means she likes me.* He took one last deep breath, then he looked at her. He was swept off his feet—off his stool—by her gentle green eyes and her sincere smile. He was nervous, but he wasn't afraid of her. There was something about her that calmed his nerves.

He said, "Yeah, she was interesting. She acted like your sister or something."

"Yup, that's my best friend right there. My sister from a different mister. We're like family. I'm even going to her sister's wedding in May. I mean, her *real* sister's wedding. All of us 'gals' are going to get our nails done at that new salon at the Pinecreek Strip Mall before the big day. Around the end of April, I think. We already have it all planned and reserved. But now I'm just rambling. I don't think most guys care about weddings and salons. So, what did you need?"

Micah found some comfort in Mackenzie's relationship with Bev. He was happy for her. He believed she was the romantic type. It boosted his confidence. He envisioned a beautiful wedding with Mackenzie. He saw himself standing at the altar in a tuxedo, watching Mackenzie walk down the aisle in a gorgeous white dress.

"Micah? Micah? Hello? You okay?"

Mackenzie's voice pulled him out of his fantasy and carried him back to his reality. The funny thing was: with Mackenzie, he was okay living in his head or in the real world. He found true happiness with her.

He said, "I'm sorry. What were we saying?"

"You asked for me, right? So, what's up? Are you okay? Do you need some water or something? Did you want to order something to eat?"

"Oh, no. I'm fine, thank you. I wanted to talk to you about... *us*. You and me, you know? We've known each other for two weeks now. We haven't gone out anywhere together, but we've met here a couple of times and... and each time has been great. Like, really, I've had a lot of fun talking to you during your breaks."

"Okay?" Mackenzie said with a pinch of confusion in her voice, her smile wavering as she struggled to maintain it.

"I know your favorite color is green, like your eyes. Your, um... Your be–beautiful eyes..."

Micah coughed to clear the lump from his throat. He practiced flirting with women on dating apps, but his compliments were never received well. He guessed he was talking to men disguising themselves as women most of the time, too. He was anxious, he felt like he was choking, but he didn't want to lose his momentum. He pressed on.

He said, "I know your favorite music. You love boy bands from the nineties. You love horror and superhero movies. Your favorite Avenger is Iron Man. You love pie, all types of pie. You're a... a pie connoisseur." He chuckled, and Mackenzie laughed with him. Micah said, "You love candy. You have a sweet tooth and that's... it's sweet. You know what I mean?"

Mackenzie shrugged, then she said, "Well, Micah, um... I understand what you're saying, but I don't really get it. What *are* you trying to say?"

"Yeah, sorry. This is my first time doing something like this. Maybe this will help. I brought you some gifts."

He grabbed the gift bag from the floor between his legs. He slid it across the counter, then he nodded at her—*go ahead, look inside.* Mackenzie gave him an uncertain smile. She was baffled by his speech. She looked over her shoulder. Bev constantly glanced over at her as she served her customers. She didn't feel threatened by Micah, but she was uneasy.

She slid the gift bag back towards him and said, "I can't really accept any gifts right now, Micah. I'm sorry."

"What?" Micah responded, eyes wide in shock. Speaking quickly, he said, "No, no, please. I've been planning this all week."

"And I'm sorry about that. I just can't–"

"I'll open it for you."

"Micah, please don't do–"

He pulled a novel out of the bag. The book was titled: *Where the Evil Things Lurk.* It was authored by 'M. Watson.' The cover showed several ghoulish silhouettes standing against a fiery background. It was simple but professional. He was a self-published author, but he polished his work. He autographed the book, staining the cover with his sloppy signature in white ink.

He opened it to the title page and said, "Look. It's a little message for you. I thought it would make it more special."

In black ink, written in his messy handwriting, the message under the title read: *To my close friend. To my muse. Thank you for supporting me. Thank you for everything. I'm so happy I met you. And I hope I can make you the happiest girl in the world someday.* He ended it with another signature and a smiley face.

Mackenzie was speechless. *'Close friend? Muse? Happiest girl in the world someday?'* They had only known each other for two weeks and they only spoke during Mackenzie's breaks at work. They were acquaintances at best. She didn't think of herself as a close friend or a muse. She didn't think about Micah at all after work.

"Ah, before you thank me, there's more," Micah said. Mackenzie just sat there, mouth ajar. Micah said, "Here you go."

He pulled a small heart-shaped box of M&Ms out of the bag. He slid it towards her. It was just chocolate, but the shape of the box concerned her.

Micah asked, "You get it?"

"Get... Get what?"

"You–You know... M&Ms... Like, um... Micah and Mackenzie. I thought it was a little cheesy at first, but it–it's kinda cute, isn't it?"

Mackenzie frowned, then she smiled. Although she wasn't happy, her survival instincts told her a smile would protect her. She didn't want to aggravate him. In a man's world, a woman's survival was often based on appeasement.

She said, "This is all very kind of you, but I really can't accept any–"

"Wait, wait, wait," Micah said with panic in his voice. He said, "You'll love this one, really. It's what every girl wants, right?"

He took a small, blue jewelry box out of the gift bag. Mackenzie immediately recognized that shade of blue—*Tiffany Blue*. He opened it and revealed a pair of mini heart earrings.

Micah said, "Don't worry, I didn't break the bank for this. I know you're a very humble girl, so I didn't want to make you feel uncomfortable. These weren't so expensive, but the lady said they were very popular with couples." He stared down at the counter and said, "Anyway, um… I–I thought it was a good way to make it official."

Make what official? Make <u>what</u> official?!— Mackenzie wanted to scream, but she couldn't say a word. She looked over her shoulder again, hoping Bev would come to her rescue.

Micah touched her hand and asked, "Will you be my girlfriend?"

Mackenzie looked back at him. She saw the sincerity in his eyes. She saw a lifetime of pain and loneliness, too. She wished she didn't have to break his heart, but she just wasn't interested in him in that way.

She asked, "Are you serious?"

"Yes. I'm very, very serious, Mackenzie. I feel a connection with you. If you say 'yes,' then I'll know you feel it, too."

"Micah… I'm sorry, but we barely know each other."

"No. No, that's not true. I know your birthday, your favorite color, your favorite music, your favorite movies, your–"

"Stop, Micah," Mackenzie interrupted. "That's not really *knowing* each other. That's just normal friend stuff. Kids in playgrounds know all of that stuff about each other. That doesn't mean they're ready to date or there's... there's chemistry. We're friends, okay? Only friends."

Micah stuttered, "Wa–Wait, no, um... I was... I'm trying to say..." He blinked rapidly while his face twitched and his foot tapped uncontrollably. He said, "I can be more than a friend, Mackenzie. I only need one chance. Let me prove myself to you. *Please.*"

Mackenzie heard the desperation in his voice. She thought about pitying him, but she knew it would only lead to more pain for the both of them in the long run. She glanced around. She clenched her jaw, then she smiled and waved at the other patrons. Some of the nosy diners watched them from their tables and booths.

She said, "We're only friends. And if you don't want to be friends after this, that's your decision. But I won't be your girlfriend, Micah."

Micah's head twitched and he stammered incoherently, as if he were an android overloaded by a paradox in a science-fiction movie. He reached for Mackenzie's arm, but Mackenzie stepped back and dodged him. She left the gifts on the counter.

"Here's your pie, sir," Bev said as she approached the customer next to Micah. She patted Mackenzie's shoulder and said, "Hey, it's time to clock out. Your man's waiting in the back."

"Man?" Micah repeated, eyes welling with tears. "Your... man?"

Mackenzie stuttered, "Y–Yeah, my boyfriend."

"You have a... boyfriend?"

Mackenzie was single, but Bev knew how to pull her out of sticky situations. They worked as a team to lie to Micah. And he believed them. *Of course,* he thought, *a beautiful girl like her could never be single.*

Mackenzie said, "I have to go. Have a nice day, Micah."

Face scrunched up as if he were about to cry, Micah said, "Wait. You should keep the gifts."

"I can't."

"Wh–Why? I bought it all for you."

"I have a boyfriend, Micah. What would I look like taking earrings from another man?"

Micah nodded and swallowed loudly, then he said, "Okay, I understand. Yeah, I mean… I get it. Then just keep the book and the chocolate. Just as a… a friendly gift. He can't be mad at that, right?"

Mackenzie shook her head and said, "I have to go. Bye."

She hurried to the kitchen. Since no one was waiting for her outside, she waited in her boss' office. She thought: *was I too hard on him? Should I have lied to him?*

Micah gathered his gifts. Although he only drank a cup of water, he slapped a twenty-dollar bill on the table, then he rushed out of the diner. He covered his mouth with his hand and retched as he jogged to the parking lot. Tears trickled from his eyes, plopping on his shoulders and the sidewalk. He entered his car, pushed the power button, and started reversing—all while keeping his hand over his mouth.

But he couldn't hold it. Along with a bellow of pain, vomit burst out of his mouth. The brown puke hit his hand, then it splattered in every direction. It landed on the windows, the steering wheel, the seat, and the floor. It hung from his fingers in chunky strands of brown goo. The puke landed on his face, shirt, and jeans, too. He drove off without cleaning himself, sobbing hysterically.

The rejection made him physically ill and emotionally unstable. He had never felt so much pain in his life before.

Chapter Seven

A New Man

"Micah!" Anne shouted, voice muffled by the bedroom door. She knocked three times. She yelled, "I made pancakes, hun! With chocolate chips! White chocolate chips! Why don't you come out of your room for a couple minutes?"

Micah lay in bed and stared at the textured ceiling, fingers interlocked over his chest. He heard his mother's voice, but he didn't understand her. In his head, he heard a foreign language—Spanish, Russian, Chinese, or something extraterrestrial. He hadn't left his room during daylight hours in days. He crept out during the witching hours for water, food, and bladder and bowel relief.

Anne knocked again. She leaned against the door and said, "Micah, I don't know what happened to you, but I know—*I know,* Micah—that it helps to talk. I'm sure it's not as big of a deal as you think anyway. Trust me, everything's okay. Okay? Hun, can you hear me? Are you okay in there?"

The doorknob jiggled, but it was locked. She knocked again. Then she gave him more words of comfort and understanding.

Again, Micah heard her, but he didn't listen to her. He saw an outline of Mackenzie's face on the ceiling. He saw her in everything—the wrinkles on his bed sheets, the swirls on his floorboards, the clouds in the sky. His eyes watered as a shaky smile spread across his face. He wasn't ready to give up on her. He loved her too much. He moved to his desk.

Anne sighed in relief upon hearing his footsteps. She was afraid she'd find him dead by suicide someday, so silence always worried her. She went back to the kitchen downstairs.

Micah searched for Mackenzie's social media profiles. He searched her name on Facebook. He found dozens of women from across the United States. He went to the 'People' tab, then he refined his search. He searched their city—Pinecreek—then he searched her workplace—Mario's Diner. It wasn't his first time searching for someone on Facebook.

And his search was successful. He couldn't help but chuckle. He touched his monitor, caressing her profile picture with the back of his fingers. Her profile picture depicted her sitting at a café, holding a teacup up to her mouth with her eyes tilted up. The picture's filter made her eyes glow. Her curly black hair sat on her shoulders. The picture was uploaded two months ago.

Mackenzie hadn't posted anything else in over a year. Her updates were simple, poking fun at viral moments, discussing her favorite TV shows and movies, and complaining about work—nothing too personal. She didn't share a single picture or update about any relationships.

Micah looked through her friends and found her in some of their pictures—meetups at cafés, visits to amusement parks, trips to foreign countries. A few of the pictures featured some men, but none of them seemed close to Mackenzie. Her relationship status read: *single.*

He searched for her Instagram account using Google. He knew how to use the search engine to his advantage. He searched: *site:Instagram.com "Mackenzie McKee."* He discovered 56,000 results. He went down the list.

As he skimmed through each profile, he whispered, "No… Not her… Not her, either… Nope… Maybe? No, wait, her eyes are brown… Mackenzie has green eyes… No…"

Then he gasped upon finding her profile. He browsed her collection of pictures. He smiled at her selfies. He wished he could visit a café with her. He wanted to travel the world with her, too. He wondered if she cooked the meals in her pictures. He was jealous of her friends—male and female. He was simultaneously relieved and saddened because he didn't find any pictures or mentions of a boyfriend.

"You lied to me," he whispered. "I just wasn't good enough for you. I'm ugly. I'm stupid. I smell bad. I'm not your type."

He stared down at his keyboard, tears flowing down his cheeks and dripping onto his desk. He sniffled, shuddered, and whimpered. He gritted his teeth and pulled on his hair, grunting and groaning. His face turned red and his bottom lip stuck out, wet and quivering. He stomped on the floorboards with his bare feet, then he smashed his fist on the desk.

The monitor wobbled, the keyboard clanked, and the lamp shook.

Anne frowned at the ceiling. She heard her son's tantrum, but she knew there was nothing she could do to help him.

Micah closed his eyes and breathed deeply to calm himself. He sat in silence for a minute, waiting for his heartbeat to decelerate. He opened his eyes and found himself staring at Mackenzie's pictures again. His eyes wandered to a picture at the corner of his monitor. He clicked on it to enlarge it. It was a picture of Mackenzie at a beach in Thailand, wearing a yellow bikini and drinking a cocktail from a green coconut.

He said, "You're so perfect. I can... I can be your type, Mackenzie. I can be who you want me to be..."

He pulled his shorts down. His penis was already erect. He began masturbating. He stroked himself slowly, pulling the foreskin back and forth over the glans. Pre-ejaculate oozed out and glistened on the tip of his dick. He moaned and breathed shakily. His eyes were glued to Mackenzie's curvy figure. He ogled her breasts, her bellybutton, and her thighs. He violated her—and she didn't even know it. His breathing accelerated. He stretched his legs out. Then he groaned as he ejaculated.

The first spurt of semen hit his monitor. It cascaded over Mackenzie's body. The second spurt landed on his keyboard. The rest of the semen dribbled out over his fingers and rolled down the shaft of his penis. Breathing deeply as if he had just run a marathon, he stared at the picture with satisfaction in his eyes. *This is what sex feels like, isn't it?*—he thought.

As he touched the semen on his monitor, he said, "I'm going to win your heart, Mackenzie. I promise, we'll be together soon."

**

Micah spent six weeks improving himself. He ordered a set of adjusted dumbbells, a weight bench, and a pull-up bar. He spent two hours every morning running around the city. He spent another two hours every afternoon lifting weights and doing pull-ups, sit-ups, and push-ups between each set.

He changed his diet, too. He ate egg whites, oatmeal, multigrain bread, grilled chicken and fish, and fresh fruits and vegetables. He ate jerky and nuts instead of potato chips and cupcakes. He drank two gallons of water a day. He removed junk food, fast food, and energy drinks from his diet.

He joined a community known as 'NoFap' and he committed himself to their movement, which was about avoiding pornography and masturbation in exchange for a range of health benefits. He believed it would help him gain confidence, tame his anxiety, and become a magnet for women.

He read fashion blogs, followed male models on Instagram, and watched celebrity interviews. He focused on some of his favorite actors, including Jake Gyllenhaal and Tom Hardy. He tried to grow a beard like them, but it came out patchy, so he shaved it.

He turned his attention to Justin Timberlake— Mackenzie's favorite member of NSYNC. He went to a barber for a haircut. The sides were cut short, the top was left alone. At home, he bleached the tips of the hair at the top of his head. He copied Justin Timberlake's frosted tips.

Micah's regimen worked. His arms grew bigger, thick veins going down his biceps and forearms. His shoulders, pecs, and trapezii were firm and defined. His abs were visible, especially in the early mornings. He looked strong and healthy.

But he didn't see a handsome young man in the bathroom mirror.

He saw an ugly duckling, Frankenstein's monster, the Phantom of the Opera, the Toxic Avenger. Body dysphoria warped his perception of himself.

"Not good enough, not good enough, not good enough," he muttered.

He rushed out of the bathroom and went into his bedroom. He adjusted his dumbbells to sixty pounds each. He played the Rocky IV soundtrack through a Bluetooth speaker. He started with bicep curls, then tricep extensions, then bent-over rows, and then he finished with dumbbell flyes. He exercised until his arms trembled.

He ran back to the bathroom across the hall, *Burning Heart* by Survivor blaring behind him. Out of breath, he examined himself in the mirror. He looked at himself from the front, then he checked his side and his back. He flexed as hard as he could. The vein on his forehead appeared to be pulsing, wiggling under his skin. He became lightheaded and disoriented, but he continued flexing.

He said, "Not... good... e–eno–"

Then he fainted. He hit the side of his head on the rim of the toilet. Two minutes later, he awoke on the bathroom floor. His vision was blurry. He felt a throbbing pain in his temple.

"He's awake."

He heard a woman's voice.

"Ma–Mackenzie," he murmured, barely audible.

"I'm calling anyway," a man said.

"Micah, are you okay, honey? Can you hear me? Can you *see* me? It's your mother. I'm here, baby," Anne said, kneeling beside him. "I was just coming to tell you to lower the volume and I found you like this. Oh my God, what happened? Did you slip? How's your head feeling? Oh Lord, you might have a concussion."

Micah sat up and rubbed his forehead. He saw his father, Dale Watson, standing in the doorway, holding a cell phone up to his ear.

"Who are you... What are you..." Micah mumbled. He clenched his eyes shut and hissed in pain. He asked, "Who are you calling?"

"I was about to call 911 if you didn't wake up. Now I'm calling your doctor. Your mother's right. You might have a concussion, buddy."

"Hey, be careful," Anne said as Micah struggled to his feet.

Micah leaned against the wall to avoid falling again. He staggered towards his father and yanked the phone out of his hand. He ended the call before it could connect.

"I'm fine," he said. He returned the phone to his father. He said, "I'm just sleepy. That's all."

"Sleepy?" Anne repeated. "Micah, you fainted. I know it, your father knows it, *you* know it. Come on, let's get you down to the–"

"I'm not going anywhere," Micah interrupted.

Dale said, "Micah, please listen to your mother. She knows what's best for you."

Anne rubbed her son's shoulder and said, "We're worried about you, hun. If you hit your head, then you should see a doctor. And... And... I didn't want to say anything, but you're changing so quickly, honey. You're eating well and you look great, but... something's changed. You're not *you* anymore, sweetie. You're losing yourself and I don't know how to help you. Why don't we visit Dr. Ka–"

"I'm fine!" Micah yelled.

His shout echoed through the house. His mother was startled while his father was baffled. Anne had never heard her son—her precious baby boy—raise his voice at her. It was frightening and depressing. Likewise, Dale had never seen his son lash out like that. He didn't know how to punish him for his attitude.

'Am I even allowed to scold a grown man?'

Micah said, "I'm okay. I'm sorry I yelled at you, but *I am okay*. I slipped on the mat in the bathroom. It happens to people every day, right? I don't feel sick or like I'm dying or anything like that. I'm stressed out because of work, so I've been a little frustrated lately. But I'm still me. Now I'm going to go into my room and I'm going to play some video games. Don't worry about me, okay?"

Anne pouted, then she said, "Micah, baby, we're only trying to–"

Micah went into his bedroom. He closed and locked the door behind him, then he leaned back against it. He could hear his mother whimpering in the hall. His father comforted her while expressing his concerns for his son's mental health.

Micah ignored them. He lay on the floor and stared at the ceiling. The side of his head continued throbbing in pain. Yet again, he spotted Mackenzie's face on the cottage cheese ceiling. He smiled and nodded. He started doing sit-ups.

Between each sit-up, he said, "Now or never... Now or never..."

Chapter Eight

The Last Chance

The door chime rang through the diner. At a booth, a young woman huffed and smiled. She patted her boyfriend's arm, then she pointed at the entrance, as if to say: *'Oh my God, look at him!'* A group of teenagers—three boys, one girl—cackled at another booth while looking at the entrance. The other patrons ignored the chime and ate their breakfast, slurping their coffee and munching on crispy bacon. They didn't care about the other diners. They were there to eat before work—or after their night shifts.

"I'll be with you in a second," Bev said without glancing at the entrance.

She hurried to a booth with a family of four—a man, a woman, a young boy, and a younger girl. She filled their coffee mugs and asked if they needed anything else.

As she returned to the entrance, she grabbed a menu and said, "Welcome to Mario's Diner. How many are we sitting tod–"

She stopped as she finally looked at the guest— *Micah Watson*. She was taken aback by his appearance. She didn't recognize him at first. She squinted at him and tilted her head to the side, as if that would help her confirm his identity. She smiled, then she puckered her lips, then she sneered, and then she smiled again.

Her expression said something along the lines of: *what the hell happened to you? And what year did you travel from?*

Micah wore a beige turtleneck sweater. His orange corduroy pants clung to his legs. His leather shoes were worn but polished—hand-me-downs from his father. It was the early morning on a sunny day. Instead of regular sunglasses, he wore purple-tinted shades. His frosted tips were blown back with pomade and a blow dryer, curly but crunchy like uncooked ramen.

Purple and thick, there was a welt on the side of his head from his fall in the bathroom. It stretched the temples of his glasses. He looked leaner, though. His jaw and cheekbones were chiseled.

But Bev knew it was Micah. She saw the same desperation in his eyes. He arrived at the diner with another gift bag and a bouquet of roses.

"Nice glasses, faggot!" one of the teenage boys yelled from the booth.

The other teenagers patted his back and egged him on, practically congratulating him for his vulgar language. Micah and Bev ignored them.

Bev said, "What are you... What happened to..." She looked at his hair again. She held her hand up to her mouth and snickered. Trying not to laugh, she asked, "Booth, table, or bar?"

Micah responded, "I want to talk to Mackenzie."

"Mackenzie's a little–"

"I know she's here," Micah interrupted. "I know her shift is almost over. I can wait for her outside or she can come talk to me now. But I *will* talk to her today."

"You *will* talk to her, huh? And what if she doesn't want to see you?"

"She does."

Bev cocked her head back and asked, "And what *if* she doesn't?"

Micah took a step towards her. He towered over her with an intimidating force. Desperation had turned into fury. Bev took two steps back.

Micah repeated, "She does."

Bev stuttered, "I–I think you should go."

Micah glared at Bev. He could taste her fear. Bev took a third step back without taking her eyes off him. She was ready to call out to her manager.

"Hey, Bev," Mackenzie said as she approached her. "*El jefe* needs to talk to you. I can take care of this customer."

She turned her attention to Micah. Like Bev, she didn't recognize him at first. From afar, she saw a guest with an interesting sense of fashion. She saw an opportunity to chat with a unique fella—one of the 'joys' of waiting at a diner. She turned paler by the second as she examined him from head-to-toe. Micah looked like an entirely different person—a rip-off of Justin Timberlake from the nineties. His aura changed, too. He wasn't meek or awkward, but he wasn't confident, either. He was a confused mess.

And everyone could see the storm brewing in his head.

With awe in her voice, Mackenzie said, "Micah... It's been a while."

"Yeah, it has," Micah responded, a slight smile on his face. "After what happened between us, I had to go away for a couple of weeks. I had a lot of thinking to do. A lot of growing, you know? I'm sorry if it looked like I gave up on you, but it was actually the opposite. I rebuilt myself for you, Mackenzie. Do you know why?"

Mackenzie shook her head slowly, but it wasn't because she didn't know the answer to his question. It was because she didn't *want* to know.

Micah continued, "Look at me. Take a good look. I'm *everything* you ever wanted in a man, right? I'm like a member of your favorite boy band, aren't I? I changed myself for you. I made so many sacrifices *for you*. And it's all because... I love you, Mackenzie. You're my one and only. I might sound crazy saying all of this, but I have to say it. True love is about taking chances. You never know if you don't try."

Mackenzie closed her eyes tightly and shook her head—*what?!* Bev stood beside her, watching Micah with a grimace of discomfort.

Micah chuckled, then he said, "I'm not asking you to love me right now. I know love takes time to grow. It needs to be nurtured. But I know you feel it. So, let's nurture our love, okay? Give me a chance to win your heart. I'm tired of talking to you at this diner when no one's around. I want to take you to a movie. I want to go to a park. I want to dance under a lamppost in the rain, cars honking at us to get off the road. I want to show you that I can treat you better than these other guys out here. The truth is: I'm right for you and you're right for me. What do you say? Can you give me a chance?"

Mackenzie's blood turned cold. She felt numb and dizzy. She glanced around the diner. She was positive that all eyes were on her. She was a little monkey dressed in silly clothes and Micah was the clown—or perhaps it was the other way around. The young woman at the booth aimed her cell phone's camera at them, trying to snap a picture of Micah for her social media accounts. Her boyfriend chuckled as he ate his hash browns. Some of the other customers looked over at them, confused but curious. Bev was dumbstruck. *She has a boyfriend,* she wanted to say. But the words wouldn't come out.

Mackenzie grunted, then she said, "Micah, I... I can't go out with you. You're a nice guy, but I'm not... interested. Okay? Besides, I have a boyfriend, remember?"

"No, you don't," Micah responded.

"Huh? Wha–What do you mean?"

Micah explained, "You don't have a boyfriend, Mackenzie. I know you're lying to me. You haven't had a boyfriend in a long, *long* time. I've seen your posts on Facebook, Instagram, Twitter, and... and everywhere. I've never seen a guy or even a woman pick you up from work, either. You're lonely, like me. I know it."

Mackenzie's face twitched and reddened, as if she were about to cry. In a croaky tone, she stuttered, "F–

Fine. I–I lied to you. But I'm not lying to you now. I *don't* want to date you, Micah. That's final, okay?"

Micah said, "I don't understand why you're being like this. I did everything right, didn't I? I worked out every day, I changed my diet, I dyed my hair, I bought new clothes... I *transformed* for you. Can't you see that? Do you need glasses or something? Like... Like... goddammit! I brought you a present and flowers! But I'm still not good enough?!" He curled his lip at her, disgusted and infuriated. He started pacing in front of the door. He muttered, "You women... You goddamn women... you're always like this, always using me to get what you want, dragging me along for fun. You're sick... You're all sick..."

Mackenzie stepped back and crashed into Bev. She glanced at her best friend, then she looked around. She searched for a hero, but no one came to her rescue.

From the bar, a man yelled, "Excuse me! I need a refill over here! Hey, excuse me!"

Mackenzie said, "I'm sorry you feel that way, Micah. I didn't mean to lead you on. I was just being friendly. I hope you can forgive me."

Bev leaned closer to her ear and said, "Don't apologize to him. You'll just make him feel like he's right and you're wrong. He's crazy, Mackenzie."

"*You're crazy!*" Micah snapped while jabbing his finger at her. "*You,* not me. You made fun of me. You *laughed* at me."

"Look at what you're wearing, dude. You look like a poser or a–a clown. Of course I laughed at you."

"No, before this. When you first saw me, you laughed at me. You treated me like a joke. You like seeing people like me suffer. My suffering is… is… is your entertainment!"

Bev rolled her eyes, then she said, "You're not suffering. You're just throwing a tantrum because you didn't get what you wanted. You're a loser. Whoop-de-doo. There are millions of people just like you out there. Go online, find a pornstar who looks like Kenzie, and jerk off like the rest of 'em. Stop. Bothering. My. Friend."

A man chuckled at the bar upon hearing Bev's feisty response. The teenagers laughed, too. One of the boys flicked hash browns at Micah with his spoon, using it as a portable catapult. Micah clenched his fists. The gift bag rustled while the prickles on the roses' stems stabbed his palms. He felt like the world was laughing at him.

Mackenzie tugged on Bev's arm and said, "Bev, come on. What are you doing?"

Her eyes on Micah, Bev said, "I'm giving him the truth. He's going to keep coming back here because you're too nice to him."

"He's not a bad guy. He's just–"

"I don't need you to defend me!" Micah shouted. "You… You… You're a whore."

"*What?*" Mackenzie responded, shocked.

"You heard me," Micah hissed. He looked at the patrons like an entertainer looking at his audience. He announced, "This woman is a whore! A prostitute!

A hooker! She'd fuck any of you for a couple of bucks! That's the kinda tip she wants!"

"Woah!" a boy yelled as he chuckled.

The teenage girl at the booth smirked and said, "I knew it."

Micah dropped the flowers and the gift bag. He pulled his wallet out of his pocket. He grabbed a wad of cash—two hundred and fifty dollars in twelve bills. He threw the cash at Mackenzie's face, causing her to gasp and stagger back.

"What the fuck?!" Bev yelled. She stood in front of Mackenzie to protect her. She pointed at the door and shouted, "Get the hell out of here, asshole!"

Mackenzie's mouth hung open. She stared down at her shaking palms. Layers of tears coated her eyes. She could see each individual tear dripping as she blinked, plummeting to the floor and soaking the cash at her feet. She understood human emotions. Anger and sadness were normal after failure and rejection. But she didn't understand Micah's intense reaction.

Micah was more than angry, more than sad. He was infuriated. He was snarling and slobbering, like an angry pit bull. His defense mechanism told him to bite everything and everyone in sight.

"What's going on out here?" Mario Chavez, the owner of the diner, asked from behind the bar.

A cook filled him in—*'that guy is fighting with Kenzie and Bev.'* The owner grabbed the phone near the register and called the police. He knew he couldn't defuse the situation on his own.

Micah jostled past the women. He approached the couple at the booth. The woman lowered her phone and cowered in fear.

Micah pointed at her boyfriend and asked, "You want to fuck that slut? She'll suck your dick for a two-dollar tip!"

"Get out of here, freak," the man responded.

Micah made his way to the bar. He nodded at Mario and said, "Yeah, call the police. Call the health department, too. That whore probably infected everyone with her AIDS, spitting in the food and popping her herpes in the drinks."

A diner at the bar grimaced in disgust and said, "I'm eating here, pal."

"Yeah, you're eating her STDs. She's full of 'em. She's a... a... a fucking walking biological weapon. Her blood is fucking poison."

"Leave me alone, buddy. Shoo."

"Her blood is poison. Yeah, she's a whore," Micah muttered as he walked away.

Mackenzie shook her head and whispered, "I don't have any STDs. I'm not a whore. I didn't do anything to you..."

Micah approached the group of teenagers at the booth. They laughed as they recorded him with their cell phones. They streamed his meltdown on Facebook and Instagram, providing entertainment to hundreds of people in the city and a few from across the country.

"Is this funny to you?" Micah asked.

"Yeah," one of the young men said, smirking.

"You won't be laughing when she fucks your dad and spreads her diseases to your family, will you?"

The teenager chuckled and said, "Shut the fuck up, man."

"Fuck you."

"Fuck you, too, bro."

Micah yanked the phone out of his hand.

The teenager lunged at him and yelled, "What the hell are you doing?!"

The girl said, "Give it back, douchebag."

Before they could stop him, Micah threw the phone at the floor. The glass cracked on both sides. The teenager punched him. Micah's jaw popped with a *thunk* and a *crack*. He staggered away, dazed by the blow. The teenager hit the back of his head with another jab, then he struck him with a hook. He hit the welt on the side of Micah's head, aggravating the injury.

Micah was disoriented. His mind was cloudy. He felt like something was rattling around in his skull, as if his brain were disconnected from his spinal cord. He reeled away from the booth. He crashed into Bev and Mackenzie. Mackenzie whimpered and leaned away while Bev pushed him towards the exit. The door shook as he crashed into it. The door chime rang as he pulled the door open.

Thunk!

The teenager hit him with another hook. Micah's legs buckled and he collapsed on the sidewalk. The other boys joined in on the beating while the girl continued recording from the doorway. They stomped on Micah. They kicked his legs and arms, his stomach and chest, and his head. Black shoe prints stained his turtleneck and pants.

His purple-tinted glasses were punted off his face. His nose was broken, blood shooting out of his nostrils and flowing over his sliced lips. His gums bled, too, painting his mouth red. The welt on the side of his head ballooned out. His left eye swelled shut while his right eye became bloodshot. One of his ribs was cracked. He felt a burning pain with each breath.

He grabbed one of the teenager's legs and tried to pull him down. The boy hopped on one foot while shaking his leg.

"Get off me, motherfucker!" he yelled. "Get him off me!"

The other teenagers kicked Micah's back. One of them stomped on his shoulder. Micah's arms went limp upon taking a kick to the back of the head. He blacked out for a second. He coughed as he awoke, drizzles of blood spraying out of his mouth and landing on the sidewalk. He couldn't fight back. So, he started crawling away.

From the doorway, Mackenzie shouted, "Let him go!"

"That bitch broke my phone!"

"You're killing him! Let him go!"

"Are you going to pay for it?"

"I will, okay? I'll pay for everything. Please, don't throw your lives away for this," Mackenzie pleaded. "It's not worth it, really. Let him go."

By then, Micah had already struggled to his feet. Covered in blood and dirt, one arm crossed over his chest, he teetered away from them.

He looked back at Mackenzie and said, "This... isn't... over... You're... You're not... better than me. I'll be... I'll be back."

Bev yelled, "Get out of here, asshole!"

The teenage girl shouted, "Bitch!"

The other teenagers hurled insults at him, too: *'Punk! Bitch! Motherfucker! Faggot! Asshole! Pussy!'*

Micah limped to his car, breathing in short, hoarse gasps. He drove away with one hand on the steering wheel. He drove past a police cruiser racing towards the diner, sirens wailing. He stopped at a red light. He shuddered as he stared at his reflection in the rear-view mirror.

He said, "You'll pay for this."

Chapter Nine

Redpilled… Blackpilled…

Micah sat in his bedroom, his bruised face lit up by the monitor. It had been three weeks since the incident at the diner. A bandage was taped to his broken nose. The bleeding stopped, but his septum was now deviated. Although still bumpy, the swelling across his face reduced significantly. The cuts on his lip had already healed.

His parents treated his wounds to the best of their ability. They wanted to drive him to the hospital, but he threatened to kill himself if they even tried to move him or if they called 911.

Aside from the light from his monitor, his bedroom was pitch black. Like a Japanese recluse, known as hikikomori, he taped black paper onto his window to block the light. Utter humiliation drove him into the shadows. And, in that dark void of his, he replayed the incident over and over—in his head and on his computer.

The teenagers from the diner saved the footage and shared it online. The pictures and the video went viral. Trolls created memes out of Micah's suffering. Some users insulted his outfit and claimed he deserved the beating. A few users attempted to defend him, complimenting his style while theorizing that he was likely mentally ill.

He didn't care about the positive comments, though. The negativity somehow meant more to him. It was all he could think about.

He watched the video again. He paused to examine each face in the footage, almost as if he were trying to memorize them. He glowered at Mackenzie and Bev. Although they didn't physically assault him— Mackenzie didn't even insult him or laugh at him— he hated them the most. As a matter of fact, he found himself sneering at all of the females in the video.

"Bitches," he whispered. "Dirty… disgusting, filthy bitches."

He closed the video and visited the incel forum. He made an account on there about a week ago. His username was 'TaxiDriver94.' He visited the video section of the website. He watched videos of death: gory car accidents, violent cartel massacres, beheadings by masked terrorists, mass shootings shot on GoPros. It had become a form of entertainment for him.

It didn't make him smile or laugh, but it made him feel better knowing someone out there was having a worse day than him. He heard a bubbly *beep* through his headphones. He received a message through the website's chat system. He opened the chatroom window.

"Fish," he read the sender's username aloud.

He looked through Fish's profile on the website. His avatar was a picture of Chinese President Xi Jinping photoshopped to resembled Winnie the Pooh—a banned image in China. He lived in

Pinecreek. He joined the forum in 2016, motivated by the manifestos of notorious incels. The spate of violence committed by incels also caught his attention. It didn't bother him at all. In fact, he had a history of comments encouraging acts of violence against women.

Fish's message read: *Hey. You new?*

Micah stared at the blinking text cursor on his monitor as he thought about his response. *Yes*—the answer was simple and obvious, but he couldn't type it out. He felt like he needed to write more. He overanalyzed his use of punctuation, too. *Should I use a period? An exclamation mark? Two exclamation marks? Nothing?* He didn't know how to socialize with strangers. So, he closed the chatroom and continued browsing the forum.

He watched a video set in Mexico. In the video, a man with a flayed face was tortured by members of a cartel. His arms were restrained at the forearms and his legs at his shins, but his hands and feet were already amputated. His eyes appeared to be missing, too. He screamed and, when he couldn't scream, awful gurgling sounds came out of his mouth. Another man sliced his neck with a box cutter. He stayed alive through the torture thanks to an injection of adrenaline.

Funkytown by Lipps Inc. played in the background.

Micah heard another bubbly *beep* through his headphones. He received another message from Fish. It read: *I know you're online??*

Micah stared at his monitor for three long, contemplative minutes. His mother knocked on his door and called out to him, offering his favorite food—homemade pizza—to try to lure him out, but to no avail. Micah nodded in determination and started writing a message. He typed, he deleted, then he typed again. Anne was relieved to hear his keyboard, but disappointed by her failure. She walked away with tears in her eyes.

Micah sent: *I'm new. I just signed up last week.*

Fish responded: *I know. I meant, are you new to the movement?*

"The movement?" Micah repeated.

He sent: *I'm sorry, I don't know what you're talking about.*

Fish wrote: *Haha I can tell by the way you type that you're new. Fresh out of the sea 'cause there ain't no fish out there for you. You haven't been redpilled or blackpilled yet, huh?*

"Redpilled... Blackpilled?"

Micah searched the terms on Google. The Red Pill referred to a political or spiritual awakening. For incels, it was the realization and acceptance that: eighty percent of women were only attracted to twenty percent of men, leading to lives of loneliness for unattractive incels; and feminism had led to massive shifts in power politically and socially, creating a radical feminist culture.

Yet, redpilled incels believed they could fight back by improving themselves and joining the upper echelon—the twenty percent—of men who got all the women.

The Black Pill was different. Blackpilled incels shared many of the same beliefs—some men got all the women, feminists were too powerful—but they were hopeless. Nihilism invaded their minds and hatred infected their hearts. They didn't believe any amount of self-improvement would help them quench their thirst for sex. They were dealt bad hands when it came to genetics.

Micah was awed. Prior to the incident at the diner, he saw himself as a redpilled incel. He worked hard to improve himself—sweating, crying, *bleeding*. But his efforts were in vain. He was rejected again. He was humiliated by a woman and beaten by young, attractive teenagers. Now, he wondered if he had taken the Black Pill without knowing it. He hated himself just as much as he hated everyone else. He was hopeless.

Another bubbly beep.

Fish sent: *Don't worry about it. You'll learn soon. I took the Black Pill 'cause some Chad fucked my girl a couple of years ago. She used me, bro. She only wanted my money. That's how girls are these days. They use feminism and body positivity and sexual empowerment to get what they want. They cheat and lie. Not all cheaters are women, but all women are cheaters. Trust me, bro, women aren't worth shit. It's all pointless.*

Micah was reluctant to chat with Fish. He wasn't really looking for a friend on the website. He agreed with him, though.

TaxiDriver94: *Oh. Cool.*

Fish: *Someone hurt you, too, huh?*

TaxiDriver94: *I don't want to talk about it.*

Fish didn't respond immediately. Micah browsed the website. He watched a video depicting a man stabbing his ex-girlfriend outside of a bodega in New York City. Blood sprayed out of her wounds and washed the sidewalk with death. The blood looked black in the moonlight—so dark and plentiful. The gruesome crime was captured on a security camera.

"Crimes of passion?" Micah whispered in a doubtful tone. "Crimes of hatred, no?"

He received another message from Fish. The message read: *I know what you mean. It hurts, doesn't it? Stay on this site, chat with some people, and soon you'll be desensitized to all of the bullshit out there. And I mean that in a good way. This world is full of disgusting people. Everyone is wearing two faces. The women are wearing a thousand. If you ever need to talk to anyone, I'm here.*

Micah narrowed his eyes and asked, "Why are you being nice to me?"

Fish: *What's your name?*

Micah typed 'John Johnson,' then he deleted it. He wrote his father's name, then he deleted that, too. He believed if he wrote his real name he would be accepting Fish's friendship. He started crying, but he didn't realize it. He hadn't made a real friend in a long time. Fish reminded him of a male version of Mackenzie.

TaxiDriver94: *Micah Watson.*

And he was correct. That message spawned their friendship. They spent the evening sharing details from their personal lives.

Fish revealed he was a Chinese American executive of a 'big' company. He didn't share any other details about his career. He talked about his wealthy family. He explained that he moved back into his old home to take care of his parents while searching for a luxurious retirement home for them. He mentioned he and his father hunted exotic animals in Africa. He enjoyed shooting guns—at inanimate targets and living things. *'Living things'*— those were his words. He had amassed a personal armory of pistols, shotguns, and rifles.

Micah introduced himself as formally as possible, almost as if he were being interviewed by a potential employer. He told Fish his birthday, his neighborhood, and his occupation. He told Fish about Mackenzie, too. He painted himself as the perfect man—*'I did everything for her! I bought her gifts! I changed myself for her!'*—and he spoke ill of her— *'She lied to me! She treated me like trash!'*

Fish sent him a rant: *Micah, you can't worship pussy. That's for those Red Pill faggots. Pussy is great and all, but it's not worth the trouble these days. Those Red Pill dumbasses basically took girls off their leashes and now they all think they're better than us. Let me tell you something, though. Women belong in two places: the kitchen and the grave. If she ain't in one of those places, her pussy ain't worth it.* (The message was followed by two emojis with tears of joy.)

Micah was shocked by the message. *Is he talking about killing girls or... or raping their corpses?*–he thought. Either way, the ideas were frightening. He watched videos of murder for fun, but he never considered doing it himself. He was curious, though. He imagined himself with a subservient woman. He couldn't picture himself with Mackenzie anymore. She was too free, too strong.

Fish sent another message: *Women have been using their bodies to manipulate men for decades. Think about it, bro. You think Lewinsky loved Clinton? She wanted his power. It's the same reason she fucked her high school drama teacher. Once is a mistake, right? Twice is a pattern. How many marriages has she ruined? These women are trying to change history, too. They're shoving themselves into everything. They want to pretend like they fought in wars alongside <u>our</u> brothers and that they're responsible for our space programs and shit like that. And they can do this because they own the media now. That cuck at the top of the food chain is taking orders from a cunt. Cucks and cunts, they go well together. My ex cheated on me with some Chad. Why? I didn't do anything to her. I treated her like a princess. You know why she cheated? Because she's an animal, like all other women, and she can't control her animal instincts. She needs to get shot, hunted like the animals in Africa. I swear, bro.*

Micah sensed the anger in Fish's venomous words. Fish didn't need excessive exclamation points to express his rage. Micah wanted to send him a gentle message of understanding, but he didn't want to sound soft.

Fish sent him another message: *I'm going to give you the truth, Micah. Don't get mad at me, okay? Get mad at them. Mackenzie is probably fucking another guy right now. She's probably fucking a different guy every night.*

Micah clenched his fists and gritted his teeth. He knew Mackenzie didn't have a boyfriend, but he suspected she was seeing other men. *No way a woman that beautiful isn't being fucked every night,* he told himself. Fish reinforced his negative views of Mackenzie.

Fish wrote: *Even if you got with her, she would have broken your heart and cheated on you with a Chad anyway. You know what a Chad is, right?*

TaxiDriver94: *No...*

Fish: *A Chad is a handsome Alpha male. Like Mark Wahlberg and Brad Pitt and Tom Hardy and all those guys. They're the guys who are fucking all the girls out there, you know? I'm sorry, bro, but your girl is getting piped by a Chad right now.*

A tear streamed down Micah's swollen, bruised cheek. He saw his reflection on the monitor. His face—bumpy, bruised, bandaged—resembled a creature from his worst nightmares. The frosted tips didn't help. He couldn't see how anyone would take him seriously. He was fit and strong, but he wasn't a 'Chad.'

TaxiDriver94: *What do I do now...*

Fish: *I've met a lot of people like you. I bet you've seen a lot of 'em, too, you just never really noticed. Let me give you some advice. There are only two things you can do to fix yourself: find 'true love' or accept the truth and hurt people. I don't think you can find love anymore, though. You're too smart to fall for something that stupid, right? You took the Black Pill after all.*

Micah blinked quickly and shook his head. He typed: *what? What are you talking about?*

Fish: *You're not going to find love. You're never going to find it. You tried and Mackenzie rejected you. So, hurting women and Chads will make you feel better. I've seen it before. You've seen it on the news. You think the Rodgers and the Paddocks were happy? They killed people to make themselves happy. They went out with a bang, and I bet you they were smiling in the end. Think of it as vengeance for all those years of abuse. For _lives_ of abuse. Vengeance is sweet, bro. You should do it.*

The most violent thing Micah ever did was smash a teenager's cell phone. He couldn't imagine himself hurting innocent people. He didn't have the means, the courage, or the strength to do something like that.

TaxiDriver94: *I can't do that.*

Fish: *You can.*

Micah sat in his dark room and stared at the blinking cursor. In the opposite side of the city, Fish did the same. Five minutes passed, then ten.

Fish: *If you really can't do it, you should try fucking a hooker. Like, as a test. If you don't feel anything or if you feel angry, then you're officially blackpilled. Then you'll know what you have to do. I'll send you some websites.*

As promised, Fish sent him several websites advertising different escort services. Micah spent the night thinking about Fish's theory. He thought about hurting Mackenzie: *could I go through with it? Am I strong enough? Would it make me feel better?* He couldn't picture her covered in blood. At heart, he still cared about her. He browsed the escort services. He found a woman with green eyes. She went by the name 'Sunny Moore.' She was covered in tattoos and her body was modified through plastic surgery, but she reminded him of Mackenzie.

He decided to test Fish's theory. He auctioned Mackenzie's gift—the jewelry—online to secure the money for Sunny's service.

He whispered, "Please, don't make me hurt anyone…"

Chapter Ten

The Motion of the Ocean

Micah gazed at his reflection in the bathroom mirror. The TV blared in the neighboring room, shouting advertisements for the hotel's restaurants and the latest pay-per-view offerings on repeat. His bruises faded to a light shade of purple, his nose remained crooked, but most of his face had already healed. He kept the frosted tips as a reminder of Mackenzie's rejection. He believed he was making a statement by keeping the hairstyle.

'Women do not control me. I don't care what they think about me. I am a man. I am confident. I picked this hairstyle for myself. I am better than her. I don't need anyone.'

Someone knocked on the front door. The male voice on the TV spoke about a buffet, then a trailer for a movie titled *'1917'* played. Someone knocked again—faster, *harder*.

Micah shook his head as he snapped out of his contemplation. He splashed some water on his face, then he moseyed over to the front door. He opened it without peeking through the peephole.

Sunny Moore stood in the hallway, cell phone to her ear. She was calling her pimp, Christopher Boykin, to report Micah's absence. Her smokey eyes met his.

"Never mind, he just answered," Sunny said. She looked up at Micah's hair. She smirked and said, "Yeah, yeah. It's the same guy from the picture... No, no, no. You don't have to do that, babe. I'm okay. He's good..."

Micah ran his eyes over Sunny's body as the escort spoke to her pimp. Her black high heel boots propelled her to a five-five stature. Her lips were plump and pink, injected with collagen on a regular basis. Her breasts, firm and lifted, were surgically enhanced, fighting for air in her white tube top. Her tight jeans hugged her wide hips and thick thighs, stuck to her impressive curves like magnets.

The tops of her hands and fingers were tattooed with bones, resembling x-rays of her hands. A colorful rose was tattooed to the right side of her neck, directly under her ear. A word in cursive was tattooed to her collarbone. He couldn't read it. The red from the rose complemented her vibrant green eyes. She looked nothing like Mackenzie—different shape, different aura—but her eyes were similar.

Sunny said, "Yeah... I'll call you when I'm done... Mmm hmm... Love you, too, babe. Bye." She disconnected from the call. She reached for a handshake and said, "You're Micah, right?"

Although he told himself otherwise, Micah wasn't confident. This was his first time talking to a woman since the incident at the diner. He stood in the doorway and stared at Sunny's hand, tongue-tied.

He stuttered, "Y–Yeah."

He shook her hand. Sunny felt the sweat on his palm. Her entire arm shook because of his trembling. Yet, she kept the sly smirk on her face. She saw a nervous virgin standing before her—*easy money*. Micah was surprised by her friendly attitude.

He nodded at her and said, "You can... come in. Yeah, come in. Make yourself co–comfortable, please."

"Thanks, hun."

Sunny strolled into the room. It was a simple but welcoming hotel room. There was an entertainment center to the left with a dedicated work area. The king-sized mattress was to the right. At the other end of the room, there were two comfortable lounge chairs and a table. She walked into the bathroom near the front door.

She applied some transparent lip gloss, she rubbed her lips together, then she grabbed the unsealed envelope from behind the sink. It was Micah's 'donation'—her fee. She charged five-hundred dollars for an hour and a half of her special 'girlfriend experience' service. A thirty-minute extension cost an additional hundred dollars. She started a timer on her phone set to one hour and fifteen minutes.

As she began to undress herself, she yelled, "Come here, hun!"

Micah stood near the front door, eyes on the bathroom doorway. He shuffled forward. He let out a short, quiet gasp. Sunny was nude. The Eye of Providence was tattooed on her sternum. She had lollipop scars on her breasts—vertical scars stretching downwards from her areolas—due to her surgery. From the mirror, Micah could see her ass was surgically enhanced, too. Her implants were too big even for her thick thighs.

Diaper ass.

In a soft, sultry voice, Sunny said, "Listen, babe, you paid for an hour and a half, but because it took you *so* long to answer the door, I have to subtract fifteen minutes from your time."

Micah stuttered, "Bu–Bu–But it was only two or th–three min–"

"I knew you'd understand. Now, come here. Let's take our shower and get ready to play. You don't want to waste any more of our precious, *sexy* time, do you?"

"I–I guess… I just, um… I–I don't–"

He gasped again as Sunny strutted towards him. She grabbed his shirt and pulled it upwards. He reluctantly raised his arms, like a dirty boy getting undressed by his mother in front of all of his friends. She took off his shirt, then she ran her manicured fingernails across his firm chest and chiseled abs. She kissed his chest, pecked his neck, then she stood on her tiptoes to kiss his lips.

Sunny grabbed his hand and said, "Come on. Shower's this way."

"O–Okay…"

Micah watched her ass as she moved towards the shower. It didn't jiggle. Her skin was soft, sure, but that ass was as firm as concrete. But he was aroused.

He imagined her as a poor man's Kim Kardashian. Sunny ran the shower, checking the temperature with her hand. Micah took his pants off. His penis was already erect, the glans eager to escape his foreskin. He took his boxer briefs off, but he kept his hands over his genitals.

Sunny said, "Nice and warm. You ready, babe?"

"I–I have… I should… I've, um… ne–never…"

'I've never had sex before. I've never kissed a girl before. I'm scared.'

Micah wanted to tell her the truth in hopes of lowering her expectations, but he was too nervous. Anxiety had a way of controlling the vocal cords, changing the pitch of his voice and smothering some of his words. Sunny grabbed his hand and led him to the shower. He shuffled behind her, feet gliding across the floor—dick throbbing behind his other hand.

She said, "Let's get cleaned up before we get all dirty again."

Micah hissed as the hot water struck his skin. He sweated because of the heat of the water and the intensity of his anxiety. Sunny tied her hair in a bun, then she joined him. She rubbed him down with soap, caressing his shoulders, chest, and abs. Then she cleaned his arms. She washed his hands and checked his fingernails, too.

If it came down to sex, she didn't want a set of long, dirty fingernails digging around in her vagina. She had bled before due to a John's aggressive fingering.

She turned him around and scrubbed his back. She massaged his ass and tickled his anus on her way down to his feet. On her way up, she glided her palms across his shins, knees, and thighs. She squeezed her fingers under his hands and touched his scrotum. She heard him gasping and felt him twitching. She wondered if she could make him ejaculate without touching his penis. She saw his ass clenching. *He's getting close,* she thought, *this might be the easiest five hundred I ever made.*

Micah closed his eyes and shuddered. He made calculations in his head: *two times two equals four, four times four equals sixteen, sixteen times sixteen equals... two hundred and fifty-six.* He was close to ejaculating, his dick as hard as a steel rod. He felt Sunny's large, hard nipples caressing his back as she moved up and down. She felt her fingers juggling his testicles. He couldn't help but imagine Mackenzie behind him.

He turned around. He inadvertently slapped her hip with his dick. Sunny snickered as she stepped back.

Micah said, "I'm sorry, I just... I, um... Can I touch you?"

"Sure, baby. I'm all yours."

Micah touched her nipple with his fingertip. He flicked it, causing Sunny to giggle. She was ticklish and she was amused by his behavior. She could tell he was a kiss-less virgin. Micah squeezed her breasts. They were heavier and thicker than a regular pair of breasts, but he couldn't tell the difference. He played with her tits for a couple of minutes, then he ran his fingers down to her bald crotch. He rubbed his fingers around down there, like a woman trying to get a ring out of a garbage disposal.

Sunny exaggerated, moaning like a pornstar. She moaned so loud that the neighbors could hear her. He penetrated her with his middle finger. He wiggled his fingertip inside of her, a look of curiosity in his eyes. He felt each bump and fold and ridge—*the vaginal rugae*. He neglected her clitoris. He knew it existed, but he didn't feel like it was necessary for him to touch it. He thought he was actually pleasuring his escort already.

He kept fingering her, but she didn't orgasm. He expected her to squirt or convulse—*or both*—like in his favorite pornographic videos.

Then it hit him.

The clock was ticking. *She's just trying to waste my time*, he thought. He pulled his finger out of her and staggered back. The water rained down on his frosted tips.

Sunny asked, "You okay, hun?"

Micah nodded and said, "Yeah. I'm good, but, um... I'm sorry, but can we go to bed together?"

"Oh. You're not having fun here?"

"I–I'm having fun, I just... I didn't bring enough money for an extension if we run out of time. Can we just... Can we go to... to 'bed' now?"

Sunny smirked and said, "Sure, babe. Whatever you want."

Sunny dried him off slowly, patting him down with a towel. Micah moaned as she grabbed the shaft of his penis. She tugged on his dick, holding it like a leash as she led him into the bedroom. She pushed him onto the bed. The timer was down to forty-two minutes and thirty-seven seconds.

Micah stuttered, "I–I'm a–a vi–vir..."

Virgin—he still couldn't say that word.

Sunny said, "Shh, shh. I'll take care of you."

She crawled on top of him. He felt her nipples against his chest. She forced her tongue into his mouth. The deep French kissing filled him with happiness. It was as if her saliva were liquid ecstasy. She kissed his jaw, then she nibbled on his neck. She licked his chest, then she flicked her tongue at his nipple. Moving down slowly, like a turtle walking in reverse, she wasted as much time as possible.

There were thirty-two minutes and forty-one seconds left on the timer.

She licked the shaft of his penis from the base to the glans and then the glans to the base. She sucked his testicles while stroking his dick. She licked it again, then she sucked his penis into her mouth with a loud *slurp*. She bobbed her head while licking circles around the glans. His pre-ejaculate was bitter, but she trained herself to ignore the flavors of her Johns. The slightest gesture of disrespect—a grimace of disgust or a quiet *'eww'*—could have put her safety in jeopardy.

Micah stretched out and curled his toes. He was close to ejaculating. He groaned and muttered incoherently. He looked down at Sunny. He gazed into her eyes—emeralds, emeralds, *emeralds.* He saw Mackenzie kneeling in front of him. He blinked, then he saw Sunny again. His dick softened as guilt attacked his mind.

'You're cheating on me'—he heard Mackenzie's voice in his head. And he agreed. He felt like he was betraying her, despite her constant rejections.

Stroking his soft cock, Sunny asked, "Are you okay?"

"Y–Yeah," Micah stuttered, trying to bury his embarrassment. "Can we, um... Can we fuck?"

"Umm... Okay, I'll get the condom. Let me work my magic."

She took a condom out of her bag. She performed fellatio on him again, putting his entire dick into her mouth. She stroked it, she spit on it, then she stroked it again. His dick wasn't completely flaccid, but it wasn't hard enough for penetration, either. She tried to put the condom on, but to no avail. She sat on top of him and rubbed the tip of his dick on her wet pussy.

Limp dick.

She said, "It's okay, babe."

Micah stared at the ceiling and said, "I'm sorry."

He wasn't apologizing to Sunny, though. He was thinking about Mackenzie.

Sunny said, "Really, it's fine. It's cool, hun. You're not the only one with stage fright. But, hey, no refunds, remember? You wanna keep trying? Or do you wanna cuddle? You still got some time."

Micah looked at her. He wasn't sure if she was mocking him or if he was being defensive. He nodded at her, then his head fell back against the mattress and he stared at the ceiling again. Sunny licked his dick while running her hands across his stomach. *Mmm*—she moaned as if she were sucking on a tasty popsicle.

'Stage fright. Stage fright. Stage fright.'

Sunny's words just kept running through his mind. He was convinced she was ridiculing him. He remembered Fish's messages. *Vengeance is sweet,* he thought. He gritted his teeth and tears clung to the sides of his eyes. He grabbed fistfuls of Sunny's hair. He pushed her head down until his dick touched her uvula, then he tugged on her hair and pulled her head back.

Sunny yelped. She sneered in annoyance. She pushed his cock out of her mouth with her tongue, then she jerked away from Micah's grip.

She said, "Hey, that hurts. You *can't* do that, okay? Seriously, I'll walk out of here and I'll call Chris. And he won't be as friendly as me. Got it?"

Monotone, Micah said, "I'm sorry."

"You should be."

Sunny continued sucking his cock. Micah hurt her, but it wasn't enough to end their transaction. She had to keep him happy until he gave her a reason to call Chris—more than some hair pulling. The customer was always right in her business. She noticed his cock was stiff again. She bobbed her head as quickly as possible, trying to make him ejaculate there and then.

Micah was titillated again. *Fish was right*, he thought. The violence made him feel good about himself. Euphoria flowed through his veins. Fear was replaced by confidence. But he was still angry—at Sunny, at Mackenzie, at the world. He clenched his fists and grabbed fistfuls of the bed sheets.

Mmm—Sunny made that sound again. She said, "You're getting hard again, babe. Wow."

Micah asked, "Is it big?"

"*Mmm.* Huh?" Sunny responded.

"Is my dick big?"

"Sure."

"Sure?"

Sunny shrugged and said, "It's big, babe. It's huge. It doesn't matter anyway, does it? It's all about the motion of the ocean. It's true, really."

Micah didn't believe her. He said, "Well, it's usually bigger. A lot bigger."

Sunny snickered and said, "Yeah, sure. You ever measure this thing, babe?"

"Yeah."

"Well, don't keep me waiting. How big is it?" she said before sucking his dick into her mouth again.

Micah swallowed loudly, then he said, "Thirteen centimeters."

Sunny laughed and repeated, "Centimeters?" She sucked his cock some more, then she spit it out. It made *squelching* sounds as she stroked it. She said, "You gotta tell me: how much is that in inches?"

"Can't you guess?"

"You really want me to?"

"I do."

Sunny puckered her lips as her eyes wandered to the ceiling. She talked herself into quite the predicament. She didn't want to guess too low to avoid insulting Micah, but she didn't want to pick a high number and blatantly lie to him in fears of stoking his insecurities.

She said, "Four, maybe five inches?"

Micah clenched his jaw, then he said, "More like five and a half."

"Really? Well, that was my second guess. My third was six. It's big, baby. So fucking big."

"Can I stand up?"

"Sure. What do you–"

Micah stood up while Sunny stayed on her knees. He grabbed her cheeks and thrust his penis into her mouth. Deepthroating was one of her advertised skills, but she wasn't fond of throat-fucking. Her eyes watered as his dick slid past her uvula. She gagged and wheezed, then she breathed through her nose. She slapped Micah's abs and tried to push him away, but he was too strong.

He tightened his grip on her cheeks, digging his nails into her face and ears. He accelerated his thrusting. Sunny retched. She nearly vomited on his dick. A string of gooey saliva hung from her lip. In a panic, she slapped Micah's abs with both palms. She yelled at him, but her words were muffled.

'Stop it!'

Micah grabbed the back of her head in one hand. He thrust his dick into her throat while pulling her head towards his crotch. He pinched her nose with his other hand. She looked like she was hiccupping as she tried to breathe through her mouth. She clawed at Micah's abs, slicing him three times to the left of his belly button and four times to the right of it.

Micah growled at her while placing more pressure on the back of her head. Adrenaline protected him from the pain. But it couldn't stop Sunny from suffocating. She slapped his ass, then she scratched him. She cut the small of his back, his ass, and his hamstrings. Two of her fingernails cracked. Beads of blood rolled down her fingers, following her tattoos to her wrists.

Sunny's cheeks turned blue. Her eyes were bloodshot, teary mascara running down her face. Her face contorted in pain. Her survival instincts told her to resort to her final option. It was reserved for life-or-death scenarios. She didn't feel like Micah was playing. She believed she was dying. She bit down on his dick. One of her canine teeth nicked the shaft of his penis. She tasted his blood.

Micah screamed. He pulled his hips back, causing Sunny's teeth to scrape his dick. He screamed again, legs shaking. He slapped her. Dazed, Sunny's jaw loosened and her eyelids flickered. Micah slid his dick out, then he slapped her other cheek. She fell over the bed, barely conscious.

"What the fuck?!" Micah yelled.

He slapped her again. She wrapped her arms around her head and whimpered. So, he grabbed a fistful of her hair in one hand and punched down at her with the other. He hit her arm, her shoulder, and the side of her head. She heard ringing in her left ear, which turned red from the beating. The blood from her gums joined the blood from his dick, but it all tasted the same.

Sunny bled from her nose, too. Her nose was broken during the throat-fucking, crushed by Micah's crotch.

She jumped up to her feet and pushed Micah with all of the energy she could muster. She yelled, "Stop! Help! Somebody help!"

Micah hit her with a hook before she could push past him. She fell onto the bed. He straddled her waist. He gripped her throat with enough pressure to silence her but not enough to suffocate her. He swung down at the left side of her face, beating her with an endless barrage of hooks. He panted with each swing. He heard his knuckles popping, *bones cracking*.

Sunny's left eye socket was broken. Her eyelids swelled, thick and purple. Blood dribbled across her lips and chin. She was knocked unconscious, trembling and groaning.

Veins bulging from his neck, Micah yelled, "You're not better than me! You fucking slut! You stupid whore! *Fuck you!*"

He punched her again. She grinded her teeth and unleashed a long, pained groaned. He swung down at her breasts as if they were a pair of speed bags in a gym—left, right, left, right, left, right. He struck her breasts until patches of petechiae spread across her irritated skin. He wanted to hear her implants *pop*.

He envisioned her breasts exploding like balloons full of blood. He wanted to hear her shriek in pain.

But she didn't awaken.

Micah panted to catch his breath. He looked down at the tattoo on Sunny's sternum. During the attack, he had ejaculated on her tattoo. His dick was still erect. He climbed off the bed and teetered back. He looked at his hands in disbelief. His bones ached. Pain shot from his knuckles to his elbows. He rushed into the restroom. He dressed himself in a hurry. He wore his shirt inside-out. He put his right shoe on his left foot and tied it before realizing his mistake. He switched his shoes, but he didn't bother tying them.

He grabbed his coat and ran towards the door, but he stopped as he unlocked it. He ran back into the bathroom and grabbed a wad of toilet paper. He cleaned the semen off of Sunny's tattoo, then he flushed the toilet paper down the toilet. He ran back to the door, but he stopped just as he turned the handle. He went back to the bathroom and soaked one of the towels in water. He wiped Sunny's face and neck with the towel, hoping to scrub his fingerprints off her. He ran back to the door.

He grabbed the door handle and muttered, "Shit, do I have to clean this, too? My fingerprints are everywhere. Oh fuck... Oh shit... No, just run... Run, Micah, run..."

He exited the room and closed the door behind him. He jogged out of the hotel with his head down. He didn't stop for anyone or anything.

He spent the next five days in his bedroom. He expected the police to park in his driveway and knock on his front door with an arrest warrant. He had nightmares of cops throwing stun grenades through his window and kicking his door down at midnight. He feared Sunny's pimp would seek retribution against him for damaging his 'goods.'

To his utter surprise, no one came for him. He guessed Sunny and her pimp were afraid of contacting the police due to the nature of their work. He also assumed they couldn't find him because he didn't give them his address and he wasn't very popular in town. His frosted tips glowed in the crowds, but no one really knew him.

In his bed, he masturbated as he thought about his experience at the hotel. He ejaculated in less than a minute. And it was the best orgasm of his life. He masturbated again and again, reliving the violent encounter over and over. He remembered every slap and every punch. The cuts on his stomach gave him pain and joy in equal measure. He ejaculated until he couldn't do it anymore.

He smiled at his ceiling. He didn't see Mackenzie's face on the textured ceiling anymore. He saw women screaming in agony, eyes wide and mouths agape. *Fish was right,* he thought. He went to his computer and sent Fish a message.

It read: *I'm ready to be blackpilled. I'm ready for vengeance. What do I do next?*

Fish responded: *I knew you'd see it our way. And I know exactly what to do.*

Chapter Eleven

Preparations

Micah shot an HK P30L pistol—the same gun Keanu Reeves used in the John Wick movies—at a shooting target. His instructor, Brent Logan, a friendly veteran, stood directly beside him, giving him tips while ensuring their safety. Micah felt powerful as he shot the gun. He pictured Mackenzie as the human silhouette on the shooting target. Left eye closed, both hands on the pistol, he aimed for the heart and the head.

Brent taught him how to reload after exhausting every cartridge in a magazine. Micah paid for four magazines—forty rounds. During that day, he also practiced with a Tokarev pistol, a Smith & Wesson 500 revolver, and a Glock 17 pistol. He shot an M4A1 assault rifle, too. The gunfire was loud but comforting. News of public shootings used to terrify him. Now, he welcomed the weapons to his life with open arms. He couldn't believe he lived so long without shooting a gun.

Brent showed him his shooting target. He said, "Great job, Micah. Got a bullseye, hit the head... You missed a couple, but this is much better than your first one. You're a fast learner, huh?"

"Guess so."

"So, which one was your favorite?"

"The M4A1," Micah laughed. "But that's too powerful. I'm thinking about getting something for home defense, you know?"

"Well, you can't buy an M4A1 like this one anyway. You can get your hands on a civilian M4, but it would take a while."

"Yeah, I thought so. Well, I like this one. What was it called again?"

"The HK P30L," Brent said. He chuckled, "Just call it the 'John Wick' gun. That's what everyone's asking for these days."

Micah laughed with him. He nodded and said, "Yeah. Well, it's great. Can I buy it?"

"It'll cost you a pretty penny. You'll need to take a test to get yourself a Firearm Safety Certificate, too. You up for it?"

"I am."

"Then let's get it done. Come on, let's see what we can do for you."

Micah passed the test with flying colors. He studied with Fish prior to visiting the shooting range. Common sense also played a factor. He filled out some paperwork, then he was asked a couple of questions for his background check—*have you ever been convicted of a felony? Have you ever been committed to a psychiatric hospital?* He was approved in ten minutes. He paid for the gun, but he couldn't pick it up for another ten days because of the waiting period.

He left the shooting range with a grin. *All according to plan,* he thought.

***

Micah yanked the mail out of his mother's hands. He stood on the porch and examined each envelope, separating his mail from the rest.

Anne said, "Well, hello to you, too, Micah. It's good to see you out of your room, but... what are you doing? Were you expecting something important?" Her son ignored her. Anne sighed, then she said, "Your face looks better. You look alive again. But... I don't know, honey. I can't shake the feeling like something's wrong. Are you okay?"

Micah grabbed two brown packages from the floor beside the front door. He took a step forward, but Anne blocked the doorway.

Avoiding eye contact, Micah said, "I'm fine."

"Are you sure? You can tell me anything. You know that, right?"

"I know. And I'm telling you: I'm fine."

"Micah, honey, there's no shame in–"

"I'm going to go to my room," Micah interrupted. He kissed his mom's forehead, then he said, "I'm fine, really. Call me if you need anything."

He handed her the rest of the mail, then he squeezed past her. Anne stood in silence for a couple of seconds. She didn't feel any love from Micah's kiss. She saw darkness in her son's eyes—*pure evil*. She crossed one arm over her chest and covered her mouth with her other hand. She sniffled as she fought the urge to cry.

In his bedroom, Micah opened his mail. One of the envelopes was full of Uber stickers for his car's windshield and rear window. In one of the brown packages, he found a fixed-blade hunting knife with a custom leather sheath. He saw his reflection on the beautiful six-point-seven-inch serrated blade. Like the pistol at the gun range, the cocobolo handle felt *right* in his hand.

Born to hunt, he thought. *Animals or people? Maybe it doesn't matter. Maybe there is no difference. Or maybe people are worse than animals.*

He opened the other package. It was full of hairnets, latex gloves, face masks, and shoe covers. He looked like he was hoarding supplies for a pandemic.

"It's not here," Micah whispered. He checked the return label on the package. He muttered, "No, not this one. Shit, where is it?"

He hurried out of his bedroom. His mother called out to him as he walked past the kitchen archway, but he ignored her. He went back to the porch. He checked the bench—under and behind—then he checked under the welcome mat, as if a package could somehow be hidden underneath it without anyone noticing.

"Shit," he whispered. "It was supposed to be here by now."

He walked back into the house, mind racing with the possibilities: *was it intercepted by the police? Did someone steal it?*

"Micah," Anne said. Her son walked past her again. She rushed to the archway. She said, "Micah, honey, are you looking for that other package?"

Micah stopped in his tracks. He marched back to his mother, anger burning in his eyes. He grabbed her arms and shook her.

"That other package?" he repeated. "Where is it? Did you open it? Huh? Did you look inside? *Did you?*"

"N–No, no," Anne stuttered, frightened. "I was just... It came in the mail this morning. FedEx dropped it off. Your dad brought it inside. It's right there, honey. Look, there, under the table."

Micah glanced at the console table beside the closet door behind him. A large brown package stood there, leaning against the wall. He grabbed it and raced to his room, once again ignoring his mother's pleas for attention.

He locked himself in his bedroom. The shadows enveloped him, swaddling him in a comfortable, familiar darkness. This was his hole, his safe space. He read the return label on the package. It was sent from a *Fisher Fei*. The address was somewhere on the other side of town—a gentrified, affluent neighborhood.

He tapped the name and said, "Fish... Fisher... That's your real name."

He tore the package open like a kid opening a present on Christmas morning. He found a bulletproof vest inside. It could protect him from handgun rounds up to a .44 Magnum. It was also stab-resistant, protecting the user from box cutters, knives, and ice picks. It wasn't impenetrable, there was no such thing as a truly 'bulletproof' vest, but it offered an extra layer of protection.

"Thank you, friend," he whispered.

He hid the vest under his mattress and stashed the packages in his closet. He drew the knife from the sheath. He marveled at the blade. The steel was sharp and durable, crafted with care in Japan. He thrust it at the air in front of him with one hand. He laughed nervously. He thrust it again, but with both hands this time. Then he swung the blade from right to left and left to right.

"Pretty cool," he said, the side of his mouth rising in a sly smirk.

He held the knife in the icepick grip and practiced swinging. He lost his footing and crashed into his desk. He chuckled—*silly me.* He sheathed the hunting knife, then he hid it in a backpack between his desk and bed.

He said, "I can do this. They deserve it."

He went to the garage with his envelope of stickers. He placed the Uber decals on the windshield and rear window on the passenger side.

"Talk to him," Anne said.

Micah glanced back. He saw his mother standing behind his father in the garage doorway. Dale approached him, hands on his hips.

He said, "Micah, son, what's going on with you? Your mother says your running around the house taking mail to your room and acting... acting suspicious. Are you okay? Did you... Did you order something you don't want us to know about? Is it drugs?"

"Oh, please don't say it's drugs," Anne said. She approached her husband, but she stayed behind him, clearly afraid of her own son. She said, "Micah, if it is drugs… we can help you. We're family. We take care of each other."

Micah could see his parents were genuinely concerned. He didn't want to arouse their suspicion. He sighed and rubbed the back of his neck.

He said, "Okay, listen… I've had a couple of rough weeks, alright? I tried to meet a girl I met online—on a dating app, you know?—and it turned out to be a scam. So, I lost some money. Then I got laid off from Carlotta's. They couldn't afford to keep me 'cause, you know, people aren't ordering pizza these days. Crazy, huh?"

Injecting some truth into a lie made the lie more believable. He *was* scammed by someone on a dating app, but he *wasn't* fired from Carlotta's. He quit to pursue his other goals. Dale sucked his teeth while Anne frowned. They believed him. They believed their son was injured by the cruel world, hit with one haymaker after another.

Micah smiled and said, "But I'm rebounding. I'm focused, like, um… Like Bradley Cooper in that one movie, *Limitless.* I saw the light. I realized what was wrong with me and I realized how to… how to fix it."

Withholding parts of the truth wasn't exactly lying, but it wasn't completely honest, either. It was a great way to manipulate people, though. Micah found his calling in the incel movement. He saw the light, but it was as red as blood. He spoke of a plan to 'fix it,' but he didn't elaborate. *How was he going to fix it? And what was he going to fix?*

His parents thought he was talking about himself. They believed he was planning another self-improvement regimen.

Micah continued, "I'm going to keep writing. I'm inspired and motivated. And I'm going to, you know, supplement my income by working as an Uber driver. That way, I can meet new people, make some extra cash, write in my car during my downtime, and be my *own* boss. That's pretty awesome, right?" He looked at his parents as if he were waiting for an applause. He said, "And, mom, I'm sorry if I scared you. I'm just eager to get started, that's all. I didn't order drugs or anything like that. I didn't even know you can do that on the internet."

"I saw it on the news..." Anne squeaked out.

"Well, I'm clean. I'm clean and I'm ready to be happy again. I love you guys. Really, I don't know what I'd do without you."

Dale gave him half a smile and said, "Well, we're happy for you, son. And we're here for you if you need anything. Just ask, okay? Please, don't be afraid to ask for anything."

"Thank you."

Micah hugged his father. Dale was surprised by the sudden hug, but he accepted it. He patted his son's back.

Still hugging, Micah beckoned to his mother and said, "Come on, mom. Group hug."

Anne was befuddled. Hugs were normal, hugs were friendly, but her son's behavior was erratic. Micah had always loved them, she felt that in her heart, but he never showed his love like that. She reluctantly joined the group hug, fear written in her eyes. Micah couldn't help but smirk. *Easy-peasy,* he thought. The truth was: he despised his parents for raising him poorly and the Uber app wasn't even installed on his phone. He had no intention of driving people around for cash. He had other plans for the unsuspecting ride-sharers of his city.

Chapter Twelve

Are You My Uber?

At midnight, Micah cruised through the bustling downtown area of his city. People gathered in clubs, restaurants, and bars, living life to the fullest. He parked in front of a bar called 'Paddy's.' He waited for five minutes, watching as drunken people exited the establishment, laughing, shouting, and stumbling over themselves.

He drove down the street and parked in front of another bar, Gigi's Lounge. From outside, he could see most of the patrons wore green for a St. Patrick's Day party at the bar—but it wasn't St. Patrick's Day. A red-haired woman teetered towards his car. She said something, but it was inaudible from the interior of the vehicle. Her shrill laughter was perceptible, though—and annoying.

Micah thought about inviting her into his car. Then he saw a young man approaching her from behind. He wasn't drunk, so he wasn't an option. The man pulled the woman away from Micah's car, then he waved at Micah. Micah smiled and returned the wave. He tinkered with his cell phone, which was attached to the car's vent.

He sent a message to Fish: *I don't think this is going to work. The drunk girls are with sober Chads. I can't find anyone.*

As he drove off, Fish responded: *Patience, Padawan. Find the girl, you will.* It was followed by a winking emoji.

Fish tried to calm Micah's nerves with a written impression of Yoda from Star Wars. And it worked. Micah repeated the process for an hour: drive around, park in front of a bar or restaurant, wait for five minutes, then drive around again. As he drove past it, he glared at Mario's Diner. He didn't stop because he wasn't ready to face Mackenzie again.

"Bitch," he muttered.

He parked in front of a bar called 'The Cave.' He glanced at the clock on his phone: *1:12 AM.* He heard laughter and music in the bar. Two bouncers stood outside, keeping watch with scowls on their faces. Another Uber driver parked beside Micah.

"Shit," Micah said.

Just as he went to reverse, a young brunette woman—Samantha Brown—knocked on the passenger window. She smiled and giggled, swaying from side to side. Micah rolled the window down.

Samantha asked, "Are you my Uber?"

Micah had been hoping to hear that question, but he wasn't prepared for it. A young man—Aaron Armstrong—approached, wearing his hat backwards. He stood behind Samantha, grabbed her hips, and thrust his crotch at her ass.

"This the guy?" he asked.

"Um… Yeah?" Samantha responded as if she were asking a question.

Micah unlocked the doors and said, "Yes, I'm your Uber. Hop in."

"Cool, awesome. Tha–Thank you," Samantha said, words slightly slurred.

"Thanks, bro," Aaron said.

Aaron sat in front, Samantha sat behind him. They looked young. Aaron could have passed for a college senior. Samantha, with her smooth baby face, couldn't have been older than nineteen. They were young, drunk, and naïve, babbling about their friends and the next stop on their bar-hopping tour. They were ignorant and vulnerable. They were the perfect targets.

Micah turned his phone off as he drove them away from the downtown area. He cruised towards the wooded area at the outskirts of town. There was a designated picnic area and a hiking trail out there. Camping wasn't permitted in the area. Fish had told him about a spot in the woods that wasn't patrolled at night. It was down a dirt road that was previously used by a deforestation company to create the man-made hiking trail.

"H–Hey," Samantha stuttered, still slurring. "Whe–Where are we? We're supposed to pick up Jerry and Keila. They're at… Shit, where were they?"

"How the hell am I supposed to know?" Aaron responded. "You talked to 'em, not me."

"Yeah, I just… I can't remember," Samantha laughed. She hiccupped, then she said, "Hey, hey, but I… I wrote the address on the… the app."

"Then he's taking us there."

Samantha looked out the windows around her. They drove past a gasoline station and a strip mall. Then she saw the sign: *Now leaving Pinecreek.*

She said, "I don't think there's any..." She hiccupped again. She continued, "Bars out here. I don't... think this car is big enough for four people anyway. It looked bigger... from the outside."

"No? Well, um... Hey, man, where are you taking us?"

Micah said, "I'm taking you to your destination. The GPS said to go this way, so I'm going this way."

Samantha said, "But you're not... your phone isn't even on."

"The screen just turned off."

"So... we're in the r–right Uber?"

"Yup. Sit back and relax. The bar's right around the corner."

Samantha kept looking out the windows. She questioned their route, then she recognized the area, then she questioned their route again. She argued with herself in the backseat. Aaron browsed his social media accounts and sent text messages to his friends. He was calm and patient. Although they weren't as obnoxious as other drunk college students, Micah thought of them as the perfect embodiments of a 'Chad' and a 'Stacy.'

Aaron was the 'Chad,' a handsome Alpha male with a big dick and pockets full of his parents' money. Samantha was the 'Stacy,' a stupid woman with the perfect body who got by with her good looks.

Micah had to stop himself from sneering at Aaron. He was jealous of his physical attractiveness, his social life, and his effortless confidence. Through the rear-view mirror, he caught himself leering at Samantha's cleavage and bare thighs. With each bump on the road, he caught a glimpse of her white panties. He imagined she had a shaved crotch like Sunny. Then he pictured her head bloodied and bruised like Sunny's, too.

"Here it is," he muttered as he took a right.

He drove onto the dirt road. The road hadn't been used for years. The ground was lifted in certain places because of the growth of the neighboring trees. The car jounced across the bumpy road, shaking like an old roller coaster. Aaron grabbed the dashboard out of instinct and Samantha held onto the grab handle above the door to keep her balance.

The car stopped after three minutes, about half a mile away from the main road. There were no stray hikers, rogue campers, or late picnickers out there. They were alone with the birds and critters, hidden amongst the trees and bushes. He turned off the headlights, then the dome light. They were swallowed by the darkness.

***

"Wha–What are you doing?" Samantha stuttered. "Whe–Where are we? This isn't a–a bar… is it?"

Micah reached into the backseat and grabbed a backpack from behind the driver's seat. He put on a pair of latex gloves, a white surgical mask, a hairnet, and a pair of shoe covers. He stared down at the knife at the bottom of the bag. He could barely see it through the darkness. *It's easy, right? I beat that other whore already. I beat her so good she probably died. I can do this, can't I?*—he rambled to himself.

Slurring his words, too, Aaron said, "Bro, whe– where did you take us? Are we... Did you... Are you lost or some... something?" He laughed as he wagged his cell phone at him. He asked, "Do you need my, uh... my Google Maps, bro? Look, it's not so–"

Micah thrust the hunting knife at Aaron. He aimed for his neck, but he penetrated his chest instead. The blade snapped his left collarbone with a muffled *cracking* sound. Aaron screamed and jerked away, slamming himself against the passenger door. His gray t-shirt was soaked in blood, black and heavy. Micah wiggled the blade inside of him. The broken bone *crackled* and *crunched.*

A geyser of blood shot out of the wound, landing on Micah's arm and the center console. Some of the blood splattered on his face, staining his mask. A single droplet landed on his cheekbone, resembling a mole in the darkness. The entire car shook as Aaron slammed himself against the door again. Drunk, scared, and injured, he couldn't think rationally.

He didn't think about unlocking the door and reaching for the handle. His fight-or-flight response told him to panic. And his panic amplified the pain. His frantic movements caused the blade to move in and out of the wound, widening and stretching the cut. His screams of agony rattled through the interior of the vehicle, bouncing off the windows.

'Ahh! God! Ahh!'

Samantha cried in the backseat. It took her a minute to unbuckle her seatbelt. She tugged on the door handle on the door to her right and then on the door to her left. To her surprise, the child locks were activated. She rammed the door with her shoulder, then she struck the window with the bottom of her fists, as if she were strong enough to break it.

Micah turned on the dome light with his free hand. He pulled the knife out of Aaron's chest, then he growled as he thrust it at him again. He stabbed Aaron's upper arm, burying five inches of the blade in his shoulder. He burst the bursa in his shoulder and cracked his humerus bone. He twisted the blade inside of him to maximize the pain.

Aaron's sleeve was drenched in blood. Rivers of blood flowed down his shaky arm, ending at waterfalls of blood—*bloodfalls?*—at his fingertips.

"Stop!" Aaron yelled.

Micah barked, "Stop fucking moving!"

"Oh my God!" Samantha cried.

The blood was clear to her now. This wasn't a sick prank. She was witnessing a murder. And she knew she would be next if she didn't escape. She lay on her back and kicked the window while shrieking at the top of her lungs.

"Help! Help us! *Somebody help!*" she cried out.

Micah took the blade out again, then he thrust it at Aaron's neck. Aaron's screaming came to an abrupt stop, replaced by short gasps, weak groaning, and gurgling. Micah had cut through his larynx. He had been aiming for his jugular, but he figured it was good enough. He pulled the blade out. Aaron slapped both of his hands over his neck and squeezed his eyes shut, like someone choking on food at a restaurant.

A string of gooey blood came out of his mouth, hanging from his bottom lip. Blood seeped out from between his fingers and under his hands, cascading down his chest. It even came out of his nostrils. He opened his eyes and tried to gasp for air, but then he gagged and coughed. Eyes as red as rubies, he looked as if he were about to cry tears of blood, too.

Only Samantha screamed in the backseat, frantically kicking away at the window. Her boots scuffed it, but she couldn't break it.

Aaron finally opened the door. He tried to get out, but the seatbelt pulled him back in. He drew short gasps, trying to inhale the cool, fresh air outside. Micah unbuckled his belt for him. Aaron fell out of the car. He landed face first in the mud. He kept groaning and gasping as he crawled away—*inch*-by-*inch*.

Micah took a hammer out of his bag. He climbed over the center console and swung it at Samantha. The first blow hit her forehead. It surprised her, it *dazed* her, but it couldn't stop her from flailing her limbs and screaming. So, Micah hit her until he was out of breath. He broke her nose with the second blow. It looked like her left nostril was attached to her now-crooked septum, glued with bloody mucus.

Blood bubbled out of her nostrils, frothing on her upper lip. She held her hands above her face, palms away from her. The hammer hit the pinky and ring fingers of her left hand, folding them back until they snapped. He hit her palm, too, breaking her bones while snapping her wrist back. She moved her arms away quickly, as if she had just touched scalding water in a shower.

Micah shouted, "Bitch! Whore! *Cunt!*"

He swung at her mouth. With the first blow, he chipped and cracked her bottom incisor teeth. With the second hit, one of her upper incisors and one of her canines were ejected from her gums. She unwittingly swallowed them, choking them down like jagged pills. Blood spumed out of her mouth in waves. Her other teeth, loosened by the hammer, were dyed red.

"S–Stop," she mumbled.

He hit her forehead again. Her brow was torn open from her hairline to her glabella. He could see the white of her skull in the cut. Blood spilled out of the cut, streaming in every direction. Her face, blushed from the fear and alcohol, was covered in it. The warm blood and the cold sweat on her face conjured an uneasy feeling in her stomach—hot and cold, burning and freezing.

Before she could yell again, the hammer hit her left eye. Her eyelids snapped shut as a *popping* sound came out of her eye socket, like the sound of wrapping paper popping but amplified tenfold. Her eye had burst. Blood, tears, and gelatinous liquid seeped past her swollen eyelids. It was red because of the blood. Some of it was runny like water, the rest was thick and slimy.

Samantha lost consciousness. Her body couldn't endure the pain, so her mind shutdown. She twitched and she snored. Micah rolled her onto her side so she wouldn't choke on her blood. He took her cell phone out of her bag so she wouldn't call the police.

He slid the handle of the hammer into the back of his waistband, then he climbed out of the car. He found Aaron about three feet away from the vehicle, surrounded by a patch of bloody mud. He was still alive, one hand on his neck.

Micah knelt down on him, pressing his knee into his back. He grabbed a fistful of Aaron's hair and yanked his head back, causing another column of blood to shoot out of his mutilated neck. Aaron could only whimper in pain.

Micah leaned closer to his ear and said, "You thought you were better than me, didn't you? You wanted to fuck that whore in my car *and* her friends, right? Maybe you wanted to fuck Mackenzie, too, huh? You thought you were a player. You thought you were an Alpha. But you're just like the rest of us: flesh and bone. And knives cut through you just like anyone else. Let me show you, my little Chad."

Aaron heard bits and pieces of Micah's rant, but he didn't understand him at all. *Mackenzie? Chad?* He didn't recognize those names.

Micah started sawing into Aaron's neck with the serrated edge. Thanks to his personal strength and the durability of the blade, he cut through his flesh with ease. Blood spurted out from his severed jugular. Gurgling and crackling sounds came out of

Aaron's mouth and the gaping wound. His eyes rolled back and he convulsed under Micah. The blade punctured his esophagus and trachea while whittling away at his cervical vertebrae. The severed tubes, the blue and purple veins, the sinewy muscle—Micah could see it all.

By then, Aaron had already passed away. His eyelids remained partially open, only his bloodshot sclerae visible in the slits.

Micah broke through his spine with another thrust of the knife and another tug at Aaron's hair. While gripping his hair, he twirled his wrist to turn Aaron's head from side to side. It widened the wound while giving him more space to angle his hunting knife. Three liters of blood softened the mud underneath them.

After five minutes of sawing without any resistance, he successfully beheaded Aaron. Head in one hand and the knife in the other, he struggled to his feet and staggered back. He stared at Aaron's corpse, awed by the gore. He had watched dozens of beheading videos on the internet—they really weren't that hard to find—but a video was different from real life.

Real or fake, pictures and videos could always be dismissed as fiction. Conspiracy theorists did it all the time. But he couldn't pull the wool over his own eyes. This was real. He could smell the metallic scent of blood amongst the other woodland odors. He could feel Aaron's hair between his fingers. *I did this, I did this, I did this,* he told himself.

He drew a deep, shaky breath, then he stuttered, "N–No tur–turning back."

His leg wobbled as he took a step towards the car. He was lightheaded, but he blamed it on the mud and blood. He threw the head into the car through the passenger door. It rebounded off the driver's seat headrest and landed in the backseat. Samantha, barely conscious and half blind, unleashed a bloodcurdling shriek. She threw the head at the floor in a knee-jerk reaction.

"That's what you fucking get!" Micah yelled over her as he leaned into the car. "This is what you people fucking deserve! You're animals so you *die* like animals! Die, you fucking pig, *die!*"

He thrust the knife at her from over the center console. Samantha's panicked screams echoed through the woodland—*'ow! Ahh! Ahh! Ow! S–Stop! Help! Ahh!'* He punctured her stomach three times. She wrapped her arms around her stomach, so he stabbed her forearms. With one of the thrusts, he cut her from her elbow to her wrist.

He turned his attention to her breasts. He stabbed her left breasts and wiggled the blade inside of it. He grabbed the collar of her shirt and tugged on it until it tore down the middle. He held the knife in the icepick grip and stabbed down at her breasts, cycling between each one—left, right, *left, right*. Her right nipple, hard and pink, was cut off.

Samantha covered her nipples with her hands, like an Instagram model in a racy picture, so Micah stabbed her hands instead. He stabbed her through her broken palm, skewering her hand with the large blade. He cut off her right index finger while simultaneously slicing her left breast again. She was convulsing and groaning in the backseat—*suffering.*

Micah was out of control. He stabbed her thighs next. And each stab was accompanied by a *thumping* sound.

Thump. Thump. Thump.

He missed her femoral arteries, but there was so much blood. She was covered in it from her forehead to her ankles.

"No, what am I doing?" Micah muttered. He sheathed his knife and hurried out of the vehicle. He opened the passenger door next to Samantha. As he grabbed her feet, he muttered, "Not in the car, you bozo."

He dragged her out of the car. It was easy because of the blood soaking the seats. Samantha squirmed and whined at his feet.

"Mommy," she squeaked out, tears flowing down her cheeks.

Staring down at her with confusion in his eyes, Micah asked, "How do you want to die?"

"Mo–Mommy," she repeated.

"Mommy? You want me to cut your head off and send it to mommy?"

"Pl–Please…"

"Please *what*, you bitch?!"

"Don't… kill me… I don't… wanna die."

Micah stared at her with a deadpan expression, then he smiled and said, "Okay, fine. I'll leave. I'll give you a fighting chance. Just wait here until morning, okay? Someone will see you."

"Call... Call... Nine... One..."

Micah walked away before she could finish. He climbed into his car and drove away. Samantha lay on her back in the mud. She couldn't hear anything, only the self-talk in her head—*'I don't wanna die. God, save me.'* She could smell the acrid stench of Aaron's dead body a few feet away. She stared at the night sky. She was blind from one eye. The rest of her vision was tinted red by her blood.

Yet, she saw the twinkle of a star. It brought some comfort to her mind. She was on Earth, on a planet with some decent human beings. She wasn't suffering in hell. She wasn't dead yet.

Then she heard the purring engine. She looked to her right. Her vision was lit up by a bright light—Micah's reverse lights.

At twenty-five miles per hour, the car came barreling towards her. One of the rear wheels drove over her head, tearing her nose off her face along with chunks of skin off her cheeks. Then the front wheel rolled over her head, severing her ear and ripping a chunk of her scalp off her head.

Micah, swaying from side to side, stomped on the brakes. The decapitated head bounced around the floor of the vehicle. He leaned forward in his seat and squinted at Samantha.

"Holy shit," he muttered.

Her face looked like it was gone. He saw more skull than skin. He opened the door and looked at his wheels. He saw pieces of Samantha's skin stuck in the grooves of the rear tire. He couldn't find her nose in the darkness. Locks of her hair and her mutilated ear were stuck in the grooves of the front tire. But she was still breathing—spasming and breathing.

Micah reversed until he reached the tree behind him. Then he stomped on the gas pedal. Ten, twenty, *thirty miles per hour*—he reached thirty-two miles per hour as he hit Samantha's head with the front tire. Her face was pushed *into* her skull upon impact, shards of her bone stabbing her brain. The edge of the tire also hit her throat, flattening her neck in the process.

She died instantly. Due to the car's jerking, the rear tire ran over her chest, breaking her ribs and squeezing more blood out of her breasts, like juice from an orange.

Micah stopped the car again. He got out and ran back to Samantha. He slid to a stop beside her, arms outstretched away from his body. He was strangely out of breath. Awe hit him first. He couldn't believe he killed two people. Then disgust infected his body. He held his hand over his mouth and swallowed repeatedly, trying to stop himself from puking.

He remembered Samantha's babyish face. It was gone now, peeled off her skull in an act of demented violence.

Fear followed the awe and disgust. He glanced around the woodland as he walked in circles around his car. He wondered if anyone saw him. The wind shook the branches and bushes. There wasn't a single speck of light in the woods. They were alone.

Micah grabbed his backpack from the driver's seat, then he took a shovel out of the trunk. He dragged the dead bodies behind a thick bush between two trees. Behind that bush, he dug a hole five feet deep, three feet wide, and six feet long—more or less. He rolled the bodies into the grave. He ran back and grabbed Aaron's head from the backseat, then he searched the area for Samantha's ear and nose. It took him twenty minutes to find the severed pieces.

He threw the head, the ear, and the nose into the grave. He doused the bodies in gasoline, then he set them aflame with a match. Like an opening to hell, fire burst out of the grave.

While the fire roared, Micah undressed himself. He stripped himself down to his birthday suit. He threw his contaminated clothing—everything from his mask and his hairnet to his underwear and socks—into the fire. He washed himself with a gallon of water. Then he dressed himself again with a new set of clothes. He retched as he caught a whiff of the burning bodies. The stench was surreal, awfully pungent, bitter, and sulfurous. He pinched his nose and grimaced in disgust.

In a squeaky voice, he said, "It's taking too long. Shit, I should have focused on acid, like... like Breaking Bad or something. Someone's going to see the fire. If not, someone's going to smell the bodies. Yeah, this is fucked. I have to end it now."

He poured water from another gallon into the grave to extinguish the flames. One gallon wasn't enough, though, so he kicked some mud at the fire, too. Then he buried them with the shovel. He sprinkled rat poison on the grave, hoping it would keep the woodland critters and passing dogs from digging up the bodies. He went back to his car and scrubbed the interior with a sponge, water, and soap. He cleaned the windows, the dashboard, the ceiling, the seats, and the floor.

5:39 AM.

The sun rose beyond the woodland, sky painted with tints of red, purple, and blue. The sound of some louder car engines, growling and clunking, wafted through the woods from the main road.

Micah had just finished pulling the leftover skin and hair from the grooves on his tires. He scrubbed the tires with the sponge one final time, then he threw his supplies in the trunk. He sat in the driver's seat for a minute and recounted the night to himself—*stabbed him, beat her, cut his head off, stabbed her, ran her head over a couple of times.* He reached for the power button, then he leaned back in his seat with his brow furrowed, as if he were second-guessing himself.

He shook his head and muttered, "No, no, I buried her ear and nose. I didn't miss a thing. No, I… I did it."

He drove off. He followed the dirt path back to the main road. He expected to run into the cops or a ranger—but the coast was clear. He cruised through town. He saw people driving to work, buses full of blue and pink collar workers, and parents walking their kids to school. It was a regular day for most people. No one knew about the massacre in the woods. He parked in the alley behind his house.

He turned off the car, then he smiled and repeated, "*I did it.*"

Chapter Thirteen

Chads

The 2020 Eric Kupper remix of *Love Hangover* by Diana Ross blared through the speakers, shaking the floors and furniture. The pillars between the tables appeared to be wobbling, too. Blue and green neon lasers shot through the room, following the beat and the vocals of the music. The club reeked of alcohol, marijuana, and vape smoke—*fruity*.

College students danced and mingled on the dance floor. Some of them looked like they had spent all year choreographing their dance moves, others barely swayed with the music. They were packed tight, sweaty bodies gliding against each other. Some groups crowded the dance floor to take selfies. Their voices overlapped each other until they all sounded the same.

'*Yadda, yadda, yadda. Blah, blah, blah.*'

Micah stood on the dance floor. He wore a denim shirt, brown chinos, a pair of boat shoes, and a steel wristwatch. He was overdressed, even in his casual clothing. A pen clung to the chest pocket on his shirt. There was a pinhole lens on the base of the clip, capable of recording in full high-definition. The hidden camera was aimed outward, recording the crowd in front of him.

He was surrounded by Chads and Stacys, but some of them resembled him. He spotted a young man with *thawed* tips—dark highlights on a head of naturally blonde hair. There were a few chubby men in the crowd, jiggling their beer bellies with the music, but most of them looked athletic. He noticed a couple of middle-aged guys, too. They prowled the club for gullible college girls looking for fatherly figures.

"I see you," he said, voice drowned out by the music.

He kept his eyes on a young man, Justin Rosenberg. He was a twenty-one-year-old college student. He staggered through the dance floor, as if he were trying to walk during a powerful earthquake. He was drunk—*shit-faced.* Micah followed him through the club, stalking him like a predator hunting his prey. They made their way to the men's restroom.

Two young men chatted at the sinks, two others pissed at the urinals. Beyond the urinals, there were six black stalls. A man defecated in one of the stalls, poisoning the room with the noxious stench of his shit. Two men huddled in another stall, snorting cocaine off the counter behind the toilet. Standing front to back—sniffling, grunting, and muttering— they looked and sounded like they were fucking in the stall.

Justin stumbled towards the stall in the middle. Pumped with adrenaline, Micah didn't hesitate. He entered the stall before Justin could close the door. Micah locked the door behind him. He tightened his wristwatch around his knuckles—*custom brass knuckles.*

Justin mumbled, "Wha–What a–are you–"

Micah hit him with a jab. The acrylic crystal—the wristwatch's glass pane—cracked with the blow. Justin's bottom lip and chin were split open vertically. His upper incisor teeth were pushed *into* his gums. He stumbled back and caught himself on the counter behind the toilet, blood dripping from his jaw and racing down his neck.

Justin shouted, "What–"

Micah grabbed his throat and struck him again. The glass cut the tip of his nose. Blood trickled from the wound, plopping on his button-up shirt. He hit him a third time. He tore Justin's upper lip open horizontally. Justin hacked and spit after the third hit. Outside, at the sinks, it sounded like he was performing fellatio on Micah.

The men at the sink snickered.

Micah tightened his grip on Justin's throat, stopping him from collapsing. Justin's legs wobbled as he struggled to stay conscious.

Micah struck him a fourth time.

A fifth time.

A sixth time.

A seventh time.

A wide cut stretched across the bridge of Justin's nose. His cheeks were lacerated, too. The sheer force of each punch and the durable steel of the wristwatch broke his cheekbones. Particles from the broken acrylic crystal irritated his eyes. His teeth were buried in his gums, barely sticking out of the soft tissue like a child's new permanent teeth.

Micah pushed Justin against the counter, fingers wrapped around his neck. Justin groaned loudly, then he coughed and whimpered.

"Fucking faggots!" a guy yelled from the urinals.

Some of the other men laughed.

Micah leaned in close to Justin's face, their noses a centimeter away. He whispered, "How's it feel? Hmm? How's it feel to have your world crashing around you? How's it feel to be powerless? How's it feel to be scared for the first time in your lucky, privileged, pathetic life? You want to beg me for mercy, don't you?"

"S–Stop," Justin croaked out. "Pl–Please."

"Yeah, just like that. Beg, you little bitch."

Micah pushed him down to his knees. He slapped him—forehand, backhand, forehand, backhand. Blood foamed out of Justin's mouth. Micah rubbed the blood on Justin's face to stop it from spilling on the floor. Then he slapped him again—forehand, *backhand*. The wristwatch bruised and lacerated Justin's cheeks. His face was red, swollen, and bloody.

Justin wept and mumbled incoherently. The pain and the alcohol tied his tongue. People went in and out of the restroom. Some made snide remarks, others ignored the men in the stall.

"Let's clean you up," Micah hissed.

He dunked Justin's head in the toilet. Plumes of blood billowed out from his face, turning the water red. Justin slapped the walls, then he grabbed the bowl and tried to push himself out, but he couldn't overpower Micah. The water sloshed and bubbled.

Micah counted to twenty, then he flushed the toilet. Justin felt like he was spinning as the water swirled.

Micah pulled his head out, leaned closer to his ear, and whispered, "You're still bleeding all over the place, you filthy animal. You don't know how to stay clean, do you? No, *no,* your parents didn't teach you shit because they thought you were perfect. So, *you* thought you were perfect, too. Well, you're not. You're not better than me. None of you are."

"Wa–Wa–"

Micah pushed his head into the toilet again. He held him under the water for twenty-five seconds, watching him squirm with a grin on his face. Justin was still bleeding, so the water turned red again. The door rattled behind them. Someone tried to enter the stall. Micah flushed the toilet again to mask the noise of their fight. He breathed a sigh of relief as the man entered the neighboring stall.

Micah yanked Justin's head out of the toilet and whispered. "You're lucky these other Chads won't leave us alone. If I had it my way, I would have tortured you for hours—*for days.* But you'll get the easy way out tonight."

"Pl–Please… why… why…"

Micah pushed Justin's mouth towards the toilet bowl. He forced him to bite down on the rim of the bowl.

"Just like the movies, eh?" Micah said, holding Justin down by his hair. Quoting Derek Vinyard from *American History X,* he said, "You just *fucked* with the wrong bull."

He leaned back against the door. Before Justin could move away, Micah stomped on the back of his head—an old-fashioned curb stomping. Justin's jaw broke with a loud *pop,* joints broken by the kick. His jaw was dislocated. Justin fell beside the toilet, laying there like David Hasselhoff eating a burger. Cracked teeth fell out of his mouth, hitting the floor with *clinks* and *clanks.*

Justin couldn't close his mouth. He pressed up on his jaw, sending jolts of pain through his skull. He mumbled something: *why? God, why?*

Micah opened Justin's mouth, then he forced the wristwatch down his throat. Justin hacked and whined. He couldn't spit it out. He put his fingers in his mouth and reached for the watch. Micah stomped on the side of his head repeatedly. The other side of Justin's head bounced off the floor like a basketball. The *thuds* and *grunts* echoed through the bathroom.

Sex—that was what everyone thought.

'Someone's getting fucked real good in there.'

"Get a room, fags," a man yelled from another stall.

Micah stomped on him for a minute. When he was done, Justin's head was caved in from the left side, pushed in at his scalp. His ear had *sunk* into his broken skull. Blood oozed out of his right ear. His temples were swollen, like his face. His head looked like a crushed tomato—*mushy*. The wristwatch was still stuck in his throat.

Micah dipped his shoe in the toilet and flushed to clean the blood off. Then he washed his hands in the toilet water and flushed again. He exited the stall, closing the door behind him calmly. A man glanced at him from the sinks with an expression that said: *so that's the guy, huh?*

Micah exited the bathroom without looking at anyone else in the restroom. He strolled through the dance floor, smiling and winking at people. To them, his gesture said: *hey, how you doin'?* For him, the gesture said: *hey, I killed one of your kind, what are you going to do about it?* He walked out of the nightclub without another altercation.

Justin wasn't discovered until his blood flowed into another stall. It took over fifteen minutes for someone to find him. By then, Micah was long gone.

***

Micah cruised down the street at two o'clock in the morning. The stench of blood stained the interior of the car, ingrained in the seats. *Bad Guy* by Billie Ellish played through the speakers. He sang along to the music, snapping his fingers and bobbing his head. He murdered someone during the previous night, but he was ecstatic, grinning from ear to ear.

He continued his routine: park in front of a bar, wait a couple of minutes, drive off, then park in front of another bar and repeat. He hoped to recreate the murders of Aaron and Samantha. He needed to kill again. He craved more blood. He was itching for the rush, *the high*, that accompanied the murder.

"Come on," he muttered, scanning the quiet residential neighborhood. "Where is everyone?"

He searched for teenagers—*any* teenagers. He sought vengeance against the kids who attacked him at the diner. The street was vacant. The houses were dark. The dim lampposts barely offered any light.

He narrowed his eyes upon spotting a jogger, Jason Stone, on the sidewalk. Although it was a cold night, the young man wore a hoodie with the sleeves cut off and shorts. His muscles were firm and toned, sculpted by years of exercise. He wore expensive stylish sportswear and he listened to music through a pair of Apple EarPods.

He was an Alpha. He was a Chad.

Micah smiled and said, "You're mine."

He reached into the backseat and grabbed a head strap with a GoPro camera on it. He started recording a video at 4K quality, then he strapped it onto his head.

"Let's do this!" he shouted.

He took a sharp right into an alley and stomped on the brake pedal. The car skidded to a stop on the sidewalk. Jason slid to a stop near the car.

He took the earbuds out of his ears and said, "What the fuck, man?"

Micah grabbed the HK P30L pistol from under his seat. He hopped out of the car and aimed the gun at Jason's face at point-blank range. Jason gasped and took a step back. He raised his hands up, earbuds pinched between his fingers.

"Don't run," Micah said. "Don't. You. *Dare.* Run."

"I–I don't have my wallet on me, bro. Take the headphones. Ta–Take my phone."

"I don't want your shit, motherfucker."

"The–Then what do you want?"

"I want you to beg."

"What?"

"Beg, *boy.* Beg me for your life. Beg me like a beta, cuck, simp *faggot.*"

Jason glanced around, as if he were searching for a hidden camera crew. But it wasn't a prank. It was dark, but he could see that the gun was real. Micah, with his dyed hair and zany eyes, appeared unstable.

Jason stuttered, "I–I don't… Hey, man, I'm just jogging. I didn't mean to–"

"Beg. Beg or I shoot."

"C–Come on, man, let me–"

"Five, four, three…"

"O–Okay, pl–please. I–I'll beg, bro. I'll do it."

Jason looked over his shoulder. He searched for a nosy neighbor or a patrolling cop, but everyone was either asleep or gone. He thought about yelling, but he saw Micah's itchy trigger finger. Death was certain if he screamed.

He stammered, "Pl–Pl–Please don't s–shoot me. Please, man, please. I–I'm begging you."

Micah sneered and responded, "You call that begging? Do you *want* to die?"

"N–No, I–I'm sorry."

"Then beg."

Micah jabbed the gun at Jason's face. Jason's legs folded and his bare knees hit the concrete. He clasped his hands in front of his chest and looked up at Micah, tears running down his cheeks.

In a raspy, panicked voice, he said, "I'm begging, okay? Please don't shoot me. I–I didn't do anything to you. I... I... I take care of my mom, bro. She's sick. And my... my girlfriend is pregnant. She's two months pregnant, man. I–I can't... I can't die, bro. Please, my family needs me."

"Yeah? They need you? Then why don't you suck the barrel of my gun here? Show me how much they need you."

Jason finally noticed the camera strapped to Micah's head. His lips twitched as a smile blossomed on his face.

He said, "So... So, this is a... a joke?"

Micah stopped smiling. He asked, "Is that what I am to you? A joke?"

"The camera. You... Is this for YouTube or something?" Jason asked as he swiped at his tears.

"This is for... for all of the guys like me. The introverts, the loners, the misunderstood, the mistreated... You laugh at us, you ridicule and humiliate us, you steal and fuck our girls... but that stops today. Your time is up. *Our time is now.*"

"What are you talking about?"

"Don't move."

"I didn't do anything to..."

As Jason stood up to tackle him, Micah squeezed the trigger. He shot Jason through the collarbone. The bullet ricocheted inside of him and went through three of his ribs. Jason screamed and ran towards Micah. Micah stepped back and shot him twice. The second bullet entered his chest between his clavicles, rupturing his trachea, then grazing his spine as it exited through his back. The third bullet went through his neck.

Micah fell back against his car as Jason stumbled into his arms. He pushed Jason to the ground. Jason landed on his back, one hand over his neck. Blood soaked through his shirt and hoodie. It dewed on his neck, chest, shoulders, and arms, like water on a blade of grass. The sound of his teeth grinding was as loud as his hoarse, desperate gasps for air. He tried to speak, but he couldn't say a word. He mouthed something at Micah.

'Help... me... please.'

Micah slid the pistol into the back of his waistband. He watched Jason from above for fifteen seconds, then he crouched and watched him for another fifteen seconds—*a close-up.*

He whispered, "Now you're the one bleeding on the sidewalk. You're the one they'll walk over. The one they'll ignore. The one they'll bury and forget. At the end of the day, you're just like us: flesh and bone."

He slapped him gently, then he walked away. He drove down the alley. He stopped the recording and took the head strap off. He took a left, a right, and then another left. He coasted away from the neighborhood. Two minutes passed before he heard an emergency siren. He smiled at his reflection in the rear-view mirror.

Pride.

For the first time in his life, he was proud of himself.

Chapter Fourteen

The Uber Slasher

Videos of the murder at the nightclub and the shooting in the neighborhood circulated on the internet. The footage spread on social media, shared like dirty needles in a drug den. The people were attracted to the taboo of watching someone die. Some users created memes with the videos for 'likes.' The incel community heard Micah's speech. They didn't know he was responsible for the murders, but they rallied around him. They championed him, welcoming him as the leader of their movement.

'Our time is now!'—they used it as their slogan, their rallying cry.

For three weeks after the murders, Micah hunted drunk college students outside of bars, luring them into his car disguised as an Uber driver. He drove them to the woods and killed them. He stabbed some of them with his hunting knife. He beat others with a hammer, a baseball bat, and his fists and boots. He forced a couple to dig their own graves at gunpoint, then he asked them to beg for their lives—and then he shot them anyway.

He murdered seven more people. He didn't record their deaths because he didn't want the police to find them.

Micah sat at his desk in his bedroom, wearing only his boxer briefs. He was comfortable with his body now, and he wasn't bothered by his violent actions. He had removed the black paper from his window, allowing the sunset sunshine to pour into his room. He ate caramel popcorn and watched his new favorite movies: American History X, Taxi Driver, Fight Club, American Psycho, The Dark Knight, and Joker. He misunderstood those films. He saw and heard what he wanted to see and hear. Fiction didn't warp his mind.

He warped fiction, molding it into the perfect model to reinforce his beliefs.

He received a message from Fish. The message read: *You're all over the news.*

TaxiDriver94: *I know. Awesome, huh?*

Fish: *I mean, have you seen the news?*

TaxiDriver94: *A little bit. I don't really watch that crap. Most of it is bullshit. Fake, hysterical, pandering bullshit.*

Fish sent an ellipsis. Micah thought nothing of it. He continued watching Joker for the umpteenth time. He performed some of the dialogue along with Joaquin Phoenix, practicing for his own speeches.

Fish sent another message: *They're calling you the Uber Slasher. They know what you're doing. They know you're routine. It's only a matter of time before you get caught and they connect all the pieces. Take those decals off your car or just ditch it. Keep it in the garage for a couple of months. The jig is up, but at least it was a good run.*

Micah smiled smugly as he typed. He sent: *And what if I'm not ready to stop? Maybe I want to be the*

'Uber Slasher.' Uber, it means 'outstanding' or 'exemplary.' That's what I am now. An outstanding serial killer.

Fish: *No. You don't want to be a serial killer. It's not like it was in the 70s and 80s. The Bundys, the Dahmers, they're extinct. Technology wiped them out, so it'll catch up to you too sooner or later. Besides, no one cares about serial killers, especially not a serial killer killing college kids. If you killed minorities, everyone would be all over that. But you're not doing that. You're not really saying anything. Just killing to kill...*

Micah leaned back in his seat, eyes narrowed in curiosity. He believed Fish was jealous of him, but they were good friends. He shook off the thought.

"You only want what's best for me," he whispered.

He sent a message: *So what are you trying to say? What should I do?*

Fish: *Think about it. Serial killers were replaced by rampage killers. They're all the rage today. Everyone talks about them for _years_ after their shootouts. I mean, who's the last infamous serial killer you read about? You probably can't even think of one from this century. But you can think of dozens of shooters, right?*

TaxiDriver94: *So... you think I should...*

Fish: *You should. You need to stop hunting random people. It's cool for our movement, but it's just not enough. Think about our Supreme Gentleman Elliot.* (He referenced another unstable, psychopathic incel killer.) *He made a statement. He wrote a manifesto, a fucking novel, and the media helped him spread his gospel. Free fucking advertising. I'm not going to tell you what to do, but you get the idea.*

Micah glanced at the backpack on the floor at the foot of his bed. He stored his pistol and hunting knife in there. He opened a Microsoft Word document. He titled the file 'Micah's Revenge.'

"What is my true purpose? Why am I here?" he whispered to himself. He nodded and said, "Fish is right. I have to share my voice with the world. I need to get on that stage... and to do that, I need to cause a big bang. No one will ever ignore us again. No one will ever see us as garbage. No one will ever deprive us of love and happiness. That's my statement. That's my gospel."

He sent Fish another message: *I understand you. Any recommendations?*

Fish responded: *Think about Mackenzie and that other bitch from the diner, whatever her name was. Think about what they like. Mackenzie liked shitty pop music, right? How about a concert?*

Micah puckered his lips and rubbed his chin. Concerts for pop artists attracted thousands of young, innocent people. But it wasn't precise enough. He couldn't know who would attend a concert ahead of time. He wanted to continue targeting attractive men and young women.

Fish sent another message: *You can go to a school or a café, too. A lot of young people hang out at cafés, you know?*

Micah imagined himself entering a café to shoot aspiring writers and coffee addicts. He pictured it like a John Woo movie, particle effects spiraling through the air as he dived through windows and slid across counters while shooting at the patrons. But the setting wasn't interesting to him.

TaxiDriver94: *Anything else?*

Three minutes later, Fish sent: *Just think about some place where a bunch of bitches go. But think about the worse girls. The ones that hate us and made us like this.*

Micah thought deeply about Fish's advice. He stared at the character on his monitor—*The Joker*—and then it struck him. He remembered seeing women dressed as the iconic character on Instagram and Twitter. At the time, it didn't bother him at all. Now, in his bedroom, trapped in his deranged state of mind, he thought of them as manipulative and ugly.

He searched 'female Joker cosplay' on Google Images. He clenched his fists as he examined the pictures. They were fans having fun, but he couldn't understand that.

He said, "You want to take our characters. You already have your own, but you want ours, too. You make your costumes sexy to tease us, to sell your 'lewds' online, but you don't let us touch. You're whores. Your time is up."

He searched for any upcoming comic conventions. He found the Pinecreek Comic Convention, set to start during the weekend. The advertisement showed happy fans dressed in their favorite costumes from pop culture—from Marvel to Star Wars, and everything in between. Most of the costumes were true to form, as authentic as the originals, while some were made sexier. He was offended by the sexy costumes. It didn't matter if it was worn by a man or woman, either. It all made him angry.

He said, "Our time is now..."

Chapter Fifteen

Comics, Ass, and Tits

Micah walked through the convention grounds, the sun beating down on the nape of his neck. Fish had advised him to dye his hair, his hairstyle was too conspicuous for his own good, but Micah decided to keep his frosted tips. He wore sunglasses to disguise himself. He thought about wearing a fake nose and mustache, too. With all the costumed attendees at the convention, Groucho glasses didn't seem so out of place. But he stuck with the basics.

He gnawed on his bottom lip to stop himself from snarling and scowling at the attendees. He despised the muscular men dressed as superheroes—Thor, Captain America, Batman, Superman, Aquaman, *whatever*-man. He couldn't stop himself from picturing them in orgies with dozens of beautiful women, tongues lashing every inch of their bodies like whips on slaves. He bit down on his lip so hard that he tasted some blood.

"Cocky asshole," he muttered as he walked past a bodybuilder slathered in green body paint—*The Hulk.*

Another tall, burly bodybuilder dressed himself as *The Terminator* from the original film. There was a striking resemblance between him and a young Arnold Schwarzenegger. Some younger women swooned over him, asking for selfies and leering at him as if he were a real celebrity. He stayed in character, keeping a steady, emotionless expression on his face. He was passionate about cosplaying, but Micah didn't believe it.

He whispered, "You don't even like Terminator. You've probably only seen those shitty new ones. Fucking poser... Just here to fuck these stupid whores..."

He leaned to his left and dodged a group of young cosplayers dressed as the *Teen Titans* from the latest live-action adaptation. They looked like children running through a schoolyard.

Micah made his way through the convention, fighting to contain his anger. He was unarmed, but he found himself thinking of unique ways to murder the attendees. He pictured himself using their props to beat them to death—smashing Captain America's skull with his shield, beating Thor with his hammer, strangling Spider-Man with his spiderwebs.

I can follow one of these clowns to a bathroom and stomp him until his brains come out of his ears, he thought. *All that muscle can't stop a real killer. It'll only slow them down. Yeah, I'm the best. I'm better than all of these attention whores.*

Through his gritted teeth, barely audible, he whispered, "I should kill you all... just come back here and shoot all of you..."

Micah's rage was inflamed by the female cosplayers taking pictures in front of the convention hall. Many of their outfits were designed with love and passion, faithful to the source material. Some of their costumes were skimpy, designed to showcase their bodies more than their characters. He saw women dressed as Wonder Woman, Captain Marvel, Rey from Star Wars, and even Freddy Krueger and Jason Voorhees.

He sneered at a curvy woman dressed in a skin-tight black suit. She was supposed to be Darth Vader from Star Wars, but if she weren't wearing the helmet, she would have looked like a regular woman in tight clothes.

Micah stopped on the lawn and watched as men lined up to take a picture with a woman, Veronica Vasquez, cosplaying as Wonder Woman. She stood five-five with a shapely figure. She showed plenty of cleavage and the bottom of her round, firm ass. She didn't charge a dime for the pictures, but she advertised her Twitter, Instagram, and Patreon accounts to everyone. With her Patreon account—a membership platform for creators to share content with their fans—she raised money for better costumes and camera equipment by offering exclusive pictures and videos, including some adult-oriented photographs.

There was nothing malicious about her. She was just a model who dressed as popular characters for her career. She was friendly about it, too.

Micah stood to the side and watched the group. He breathed deeply through his nose and scowled at Veronica. He believed she would fail if he quizzed her about Wonder Woman. As a matter of fact, he believed every *beautiful* person at the convention would fail if he quizzed them about their costumes. He convinced himself that they weren't really interested in the source material. They were there to manipulate men—*bluepilled virgins*.

"Selling your bodies for tips," he muttered. He looked at the line of men and, under his breath, he said, "Look at all of you simps, giving her what she wants. Money, attention, self-worth... Selling your pride for a couple of seconds of attention. She's not going to fuck any of you, you damn retards. You should all hang yourselves. Kill yourselves or open your eyes and–"

"You got a problem?" Veronica asked.

Micah squinted at her, baffled. *Did I say all of that out loud? Did she hear me?*–he thought. He considered running off, then he noticed the audience of men watching him. He had flashbacks to the incident at the diner. He refused to allow another woman to humiliate him again. He scoffed at her and marched forward.

"You talkin' to me?" he asked, mimicking Travis Bickle from Taxi Driver.

Veronica huffed, then she said, "Yeah, I'm talking to you. You okay? We see you standing over there, muttering and mad-dogging. You got a problem?"

"You know what? I *do* have a problem."

"Okay, so... walk away."

"Are you telling me what to do?"

"I'm giving you some friendly advice, buddy. Security can be here in seconds and I'd rather not spoil my day dealing with you. You got a problem with me, you hate my guts...*great,* you're not the first guy to try to troll me at one of my appearances. Save yourself the embarrassment and just go."

Micah laughed as he approached her. Veronica took a step back while her professional photographer, a middle-aged man, stepped forward. She acted tough, she needed thick skin to survive in the business, but she knew the dangers of provoking unhinged men. The crowd whispered amongst themselves—*who is that guy? A troll? What's he doing here?*

The photographer said, "We don't want any problems. Everyone's just trying to have some fun. Can we de-escalate this? Please?"

Ignoring him, Micah glared at Veronica and said, "Look at yourself. *Listen* to yourself. One of your 'appearances?' Really? You think you're hot shit. Your ego is so fucking big you actually think you have an army of trolls obsessed with you. Well, listen up: I don't know who you are. I've never—*never*—heard of you."

"Cool," Veronica said as she took another step back. "Can you please leave us alone?"

"Oh, I like that. 'Please.' You still have that snobby attitude, but you're starting to learn some manners. You're not as tough as you pretend to be."

"Learn some manners? Bro, what do you–"

"*Don't* call me 'bro,' woman," Micah interrupted, wagging his finger at her. The photographer stepped between them with his hands up, still carrying the camera. Micah continued, "That's for us. That's for *men*. That's what we call each other, you understand? You're already standing here trying to steal our characters, I'm not going to let you steal our language, too. It's like... like... like everything else you try to take. I hate—*I hate*—hearing girls tell people to 'suck my dick.' I hate watching you dress as characters you can barely name. I hate hearing you talk about life and politics and all that bullshit when you've spent the last few millenniums trapped in the kitchen. We give you a little freedom and you *immediately* try to overpower us."

"You're sick," Veronica said. "You need to get help. Talk to someone. Get out of your little bubble and enter the real world. Don't be another loser incel."

"Loser incel?" Micah repeated, eyes and smile wide.

He glanced around, as if to say: *are you guys hearing this?* But the audience didn't agree with him. They were repulsed by his hateful speech. Some of them recorded his rant on their cell phones. Others left out of fear for their safety.

"He's crazy," a man whispered in the line.

"Dude's got problems," someone else said in a hushed tone.

A woman said, "He's taking this way too seriously."

From behind the group, hiding behind his friends, a young man yelled, "Fucking incel!"

"Loser!" another man shouted.

"Get out of here already!" another woman yelled from behind the group.

Micah chuckled in disbelief, then he said, "You idiots. She's *using* you! You think she's going to fuck you just because she let you take a picture with her? You're selling your souls for comics, ass, and tits. Open your eyes."

The photographer beckoned to another man and said, "Call security."

"God, you have to be kidding me. Security? Really? You're all a bunch of pussies. All of you guys out here—and you Beckys, too—you're just giving her more power for doing nothing more than existing."

(A *'Becky'* was an incel term used to refer to average women.)

A woman shouted, "Leave! Leave!"

The audience started chanting with her: *'Leave! Leave! Leave!'*

Some of them hurled insults at him: *'Idiot! Asshole! Incel!'*

Veronica and the photographer tried to keep the crowd calm. They didn't want to lead a mob into a violent altercation. They were there to have fun and socialize, advertise their social media accounts and websites, and build a network of likeminded contacts.

Micah's blood boiled, fingernails deep in his palms. He stormed away before security guards could arrive at the scene. He bulldozed past the other attendees, pushing everyone in his path. They yelled at him, but no one could stop him.

He sat in the driver's seat of his car and grabbed the pistol from under his seat. He gazed at it, as if he were hypnotized by the weapon. He heard echoes of gunfire and women screaming at the back of his head. He reached for the door handle, then he stopped. He spotted a guard jogging down the sidewalk, clearly searching for someone—*for him.*

His eyes on the guard, he tucked the pistol under his seat and put on his seatbelt. He said, "No, not here. It's too busy, too secure. They'd stop me before I could even kill a handful of people. I don't even… Jesus Christ, I don't even have my vest. What the hell was I thinking?" As he reversed out of his parking space, he whispered, "You need to calm down, Micah. Don't let these whores get to you. Emotions lead to mistakes, mistakes lead to embarrassment. Don't embarrass yourself. This is for the movement."

He drove through town, searching for the perfect target. He examined schools—elementary, middle, and high schools—but he didn't want to copy past spree killers. He stopped at a college, but he drove away upon spotting the campus police. He walked through enclosed shopping malls and large parks. He thought about visiting an amusement park, but he knew security was strict in each one. He couldn't waltz in without walking through a metal detector.

"I can do better," he whispered. "I have to go out with a bang…"

Chapter Sixteen

The New Plan

Micah sat at his desk, browsing the Fuck-Less forums. He was bored of it. *All talk, no action,* he thought. He read about spree killers, serial killers, and rampage killers, searching for a spark of inspiration. He was already legendary amongst incel groups as the *Uber Slasher*, but they didn't know Micah's true identity. He wanted to reveal himself by going out in a blaze of glory.

Frustrated, he minimized the web browser and started playing video games. He played Grand Theft Auto V, Postal 2, and Hatred. He played for hours, killing non-playable characters in every way imaginable, but he felt nothing. The video games couldn't inspire him, either. Movies, video games, *fiction*—none of it made a killer commit murder.

He went back to the internet. He browsed news sites, reading about the awful things people did to each other. It fascinated him. His eyes widened as he spotted an advertisement for iHop. It promoted an all-you-can-eat-pancakes offer. He didn't care about the food, but the advertisement sparked an explosion of memories in his mind.

"Mario's Diner," he said. "Mackenzie... Beverly..."

He remembered his conversations with Mackenzie. His eyes filled with tears as he reminisced about their good times together. He looked at his hand. His palm turned warm as he remembered their handshake. Tears dripped from his eyes as he blinked. He shook his head, clenched his fist, and gritted his teeth.

Eyes clenched shut, he said, "You don't love her, Micah. You don't love her. You *don't* love her. She lied to you. She treated you like shit. You have to get revenge. You know what to do, so do it. Don't be a cuck, don't be a simp. Do it. *Do it.*"

He opened his eyes and started typing. He searched for nail salons at the Pinecreek Strip Mall. He found a shop called '*Lee's Nails.*' He browsed the website until he reached the 'Reservations' page. There was a message at the top of the page.

The message read: *Due to a private party, Lee's Nails will be closed from 4:00 PM to 7:00 PM on April 22nd, 2020. Feel free to schedule a meeting with one of our specialists during any other time. Have a pleasant day!*

Micah said, "Private party. That's Beverly's sister's wedding party. It has to be. You're all getting your 'nails done' there, aren't you? You said that when we met... I've got you in my crosshairs, you dirty bitches. Oh, yeah, you're mine... all mine..."

He searched the immediate area for schools— particularly, *high schools*. He wanted to kill young students because of what the teenagers did to him at the diner. To his utter disappointment, the closest school—a private high school—was three miles away. The closest public school was five miles away.

He didn't think he could cover that much ground between his planned attacks.

"It's impossible," he whispered. "As soon as I start, the police will be all over me. If I start at the school, I can't reach the salon in time. If I start at the salon, I can't reach the high school. Shit, I'd need a miracle."

He scratched his hair and mumbled indistinctly to himself, sorting through his options and assessing the risks.

He said, "No, it's too dangerous. I can't gamble with this. I get one shot and one shot only. Back to the drawing board."

He measured the distance between the convention center and the nail salon—*two and a half miles.* The Pinecreek Comic Convention was scheduled to end before the private party at the nail salon, though. He searched the stores at the Pinecreek Strip Mall. There was a liquor store, a burger restaurant, a sushi restaurant, a laundromat, an insurance office, and a grocery store.

"They're right there, right next door, but they'll run or close the doors as soon as they hear me coming," he rationalized. "It has to be separate locations. They can't see me coming."

He groaned in frustration. He found himself staring at the iHop advertisement again. The idea hit him. He measured the distance between Lee's Salon and Mario's Diner.

Zero-point-eight miles away.

Accounting for red lights and traffic, it was only a four-minute drive away.

He said, "This'll work. I've only got a week to get ready."

He sent Fish a message: *I'm ready for the final stage. I've got my targets. I just need to finish up some final preparations. You wanna hear about it?*

Fifteen minutes passed without a response. Micah sent him another message comprised of three question marks. Thirty minutes passed and, yet again, there was no response.

Micah sent him a third message: *Hey, man, you busy? It's cool if you are. Just call me when you're free, okay?*

He left his phone number after the message. He used a live operating system called Tails to access the deep web through a flash drive. He visited a marketplace selling illegal drugs, firearms, and other specialty items. His virtual wallet was loaded with digital, untraceable currency. He browsed the firearms. He wanted a powerful rifle, but he didn't want to spend all of his money on one item.

"Fish said his dad hunts," he said to himself. "I can get some guns from him."

He found a seller who specialized in body armor. His eyes glowed with sparks of deviance as dangerous ideas ran through his mind. *I'd be unstoppable,* he thought. He purchased a Kevlar bulletproof vest. It was much more durable than the gift Fish had sent him. Then he bought a set of custom black AR500 steel shoulder pads, kneepads, a chest plate, and a plate for his back. He also purchased a matte ballistic helmet constructed from durable composite materials. He spent his entire savings on the supplies.

He received a message from Fish: *I don't know what you're talking about.*

Micah furrowed his brow and huffed. He sent: *What? I'm talking about the big 'event.' You said I needed to step it up. So, I'm ready to step up. I know my targets. I'm getting geared up right now. Btw, I need to ask you for a favor.*

Fish: *I don't know what you're talking about.*

"What the fuck?" Micah whispered, awed.

He responded: *Dude, what's up with you? You're the one that told me to get ready for this.*

Fish sent: *I didn't tell you anything.* Before Micah could respond, he sent another message: *Listen, we can't talk about any of this crap on here. Stop trying to drag me down with you. Do whatever you're going to do. I don't know anything.*

Micah sent him another message: *You're pussying out?*

Fish didn't respond.

TaxiDriver94: *Hey, call me. Let's talk about it in private.*

There was no response.

TaxiDriver94: *You're acting like them. For your own good, don't do this. Seriously, bro.*

Yet again, no response.

Micah sat in silence and stared at his monitor for an hour. He waited for Fish's response, but it never arrived. He tried to understand Fish's bizarre behavior. *Maybe he's being watched by the FBI, maybe he's a coward, maybe he's a traitor,* he thought. He wanted to punch a hole through his monitor, but he didn't want to alarm his parents.

"This isn't over," he whispered.

***

The doorbell echoed through the house. Anne answered the door. She was greeted by the friendly mailman, Malcolm Fox, who had rolled a dolly with a package to the bottom of the porch steps.

As Anne signed for the package, Micah squeezed past her and said, "That's for me. I can carry it into the house."

"I can help you with that, son," Malcolm said.

"No, no. You've done enough. Thank you."

"Are you sure? It's a little heavy."

"Yeah, of course. I can handle it."

Micah lifted the box. It weighed over sixty pounds, but it was easy for him to carry. He smirked at his mother as she stepped aside.

"Have a nice day!" he shouted as he entered the house.

Anne smiled at the mailman and said, "Thank you. Please have a nice day." She closed the door and hurried down the hall, following Micah to his bedroom. She asked, "Micah, hun, what is that? Did you buy a–"

Micah walked into his room and kicked the door shut behind him, slamming it in Anne's face. Anne sighed in disappointment as she heard the lock *click*.

Micah opened the package on his bed. It was the armor he had purchased on the deep web. The plates of AR500 steel were one-fourth-inch thick. He put on the Kevlar vest, then he strapped the chest and back plates to his torso. He secured the kneepads to his knees and shoulder pads to his shoulders. Then he strapped the helmet to his head.

He took multiple selfies with a wide-angle camera. He posed with a serious, steady expression in each picture, but he couldn't help but smile between shots. He was ecstatic. He felt like a child trying on the Halloween costume of his dreams for the first time. The custom suit of armor was heavy, though. His movements were restricted. He couldn't breathe well, either. Sweat dripped across his forehead and soaked his armpits.

"I just need… some practice."

He removed the armor, then he sat on his bed and caught his breath. He was worried about his mobility with the armor, but he refused to change his plans. April 22nd was marked on his calendar. It was only four days away.

He went to his desk and opened a Microsoft Word document titled: *Micah's Revenge.* He had already written over thirty-five thousand words for his manifesto. The beginning covered his life, discussing his happy childhood, his lonely teenage years, and his pitiful adult life. He accused his parents of being deceitful and hindering his growth. He wrote about bullies, including the teenagers from the diner. And he ranted about the women in his life—those who rejected him. He claimed women deprived him of happiness for their sick pleasure and he condemned the men who refused to help him.

Now, he wrote about politics. He attacked politicians from across the spectrum, assaulting manipulative, self-serving politicians with a flurry of words. The President of the United States wasn't spared. Leaders from other countries also landed in his textual onslaught. He chastised the rich for hoarding all of the wealth and he criticized the poor for accepting poverty and burdening the system. He took jabs at corporations and Wall Street.

Then, he wrote about Mackenzie. He *blamed* her for his actions, but he also *thanked* her for opening his eyes. He typed thousands of words about her, covering their entire relationship while also making assumptions about her. He claimed she manipulated him because she was a sadist, she sold her body for 'tips' using the diner as a way to find clients, and sexually transmitted diseases infected her blood.

He finished his manifesto by detailing his plans, explaining his goals, and once again, describing the reasons for his actions—*women, women, those fucking women!* He explained that he hoped his actions would usher in a new world. He envisioned a society where women served men as lovely housewives or forfeited their freedom to work as sex slaves. If he survived, he hoped he would be crowned King of this world, watching the slaves from a tower while women sucked his dick and toes.

The manifesto was 105,249 words long.

He printed two copies of the 205-page document. He had to add paper to the printer several times to keep it going, and he had to change the ink cartridge between each copy. He planned on keeping one in his bedroom and sending the other to a local news outlet.

Staring at the cover page, reading the title over and over, he said, "It's a masterpiece. They'll be reading this for years."

He visited Fuck-Less again. He sent Fish another message. He asked to borrow a gun from Fish's father for a hunting excursion. He immediately received an error message: *You are blocked from contacting this member.* Fish's username disappeared from his contact list on the website. He stopped smiling, confidence replaced by anger.

"You fucking simp!" he shouted. He jumped up to his feet, launching the chair back until it hit the closet. Pacing back and forth in front of his desk, he said, "I knew you weren't a man of your word. You're not a man at all. You let your bitch walk all over you. You let her *cuck* you. You talk big, but you're small. You're a small, pathetic boy. Well, *Fish,* you fucked with the wrong shark. I know where you live. I know…"

His eyes widened and he stopped pacing, as if he had just realized what he had said. He rushed to the closet, pushing the chair towards the door. He looked through the envelopes and packages on the closet floor. He found the package from Fisher Fei. He read the address again and again.

He repeated, "I know where you live."

Chapter Seventeen

Fish

Micah rang the doorbell, then he knocked on the front door. Two young girls on bicycles with training wheels rang their bells and giggled as they followed their mothers down the sidewalk. An SUV rolled by the house, then a pickup truck followed. At four o'clock in the afternoon, the sun blanketed the neighborhood with a welcomed warmth. The aroma of flowers and pie wafted through the street.

The door cracked open a foot. Carrie Fei, a fifty-six-year-old woman, peeked out onto the porch through the crack. Her short, permed hair was dyed black. She concealed the wrinkles around her eyes and lips with makeup, but the creases and grooves were still obvious. She stood about five feet tall, although her slippers appeared to add about half an inch to her stature.

The woman wore a housedress with a floral pattern and a pink apron. The apron had a cartoonish pig on it. Under the pig, a message read: *World's Best Cook*. Micah grinned at her, trying to blend in with the unusually happy atmosphere in the neighborhood. Carrie didn't recognize him as a neighbor. He didn't look trustworthy to her, either.

She asked, "May I help you?"

"You must be the beautiful, talented, *lovely* Mrs. Fei. Am I right?"

"May I... help you?"

"Oh, straight to the point, I like it. They did say you were a straight shooter."

"They?"

"I'm sorry, *'he.'* Your son, Fisher Fei, he talks about you all the time. I'm his friend, you see? I guess some would call us *best* friends. So, I'm just here to ask a simple question. Maybe you've heard it before, but I'm absolutely serious."

Very slowly, Carrie nodded once while staring at him with a set of dumbfounded eyes.

Micah leaned closer to the door and, with his toothy grin, he asked, "Can Fisher come out and play?"

He sounded like a boy to Carrie, but his young face and dyed hair made him look like a college student—an eccentric, *confused* college student. She scanned him from head to toe, leading to more confusion. A backpack slung over his shoulders, he wore navy coveralls, black gloves, and steel-toe boots. He somehow looked young and old, casual and professional, at the same time.

Carrie stuttered, "I–I'll... What's your name?"

"Micah Watson, ma'am."

"Micah... I'll go ask Fisher if he wants to see you."

Before Carrie could close the door, Micah put his foot in the doorway and stopped her. He said, "Well, why don't I just come inside and surprise him?"

"No, I'm sorry, you can't. Please move your foot, sir."

"I don't have time for games."

"E–Excuse me?"

Micah smiled and said, "I have an appointment at the nail salon today. I'd really appreciate it if you got out of my way."

Carrie shook her head slowly. She pressed her shoulder against the door and tried to close it, but she couldn't move Micah's foot. Micah groaned in frustration, tired of wasting his time. He didn't want Carrie to alarm Fisher, either. He sought an advantage over him. He expected to find a crazed lunatic in the house—a killer, like himself.

Micah shrugged and said, "At least I know he's home."

He tackled the door and forced his way into the house. The edge of the door hit Carrie's chest and face, breaking a rib, slicing her lips open, and cracking her teeth. She fell on her ass, mouth open and eyes shut. Blood dripped from her chin and plopped on her apron as she moaned in pain. She whimpered as she heard the door's locks—*click! Click!* She opened her eyes upon hearing the zipper of Micah's backpack.

With pure terror in her eyes—pupils dilated, upper eyelids raised, lower eyelids tensed—she shrieked.

Micah pulled the sheathed hunting knife out of his backpack, then he unsheathed the blade. He ran forward while Carrie crab-walked back down the hall, hands and feet sliding on the floorboards. Micah thrust the knife into her lower abdomen, directly through her bellybutton. Through her clenched teeth, she shrieked again. Micah stabbed her below the ribs—through the cartoonish pig on her apron—and punctured her stomach.

Carrie fell back against the floor, grimacing while holding her breath. A burning pain traveled across her torso, like mist rolling slowly over a lake. The pain was debilitating, causing her to breathe in short gasps. The bile from her stomach flooded her peritoneal cavity, creating a septic infection in her body. Then blood from her wound poured into her punctured stomach. She felt an unsettling pressure inside of her, as if her organs were about to explode.

Micah crouched in front of her and said, "Wow, look at you. You look like you're in pain—in *so* much pain. I don't know if you're playing it up, but it's beautiful. You ever act before? Movies? Plays? Anything?" Carrie grunted and groaned. As he cleaned the blade with her apron, Micah said, "Your husband... Is he home? Will he be home soon? Hello, can you hear–"

Carrie kicked him. It was a weak kick, but it was enough to knock him off his balance. He landed on his ass, chuckling. Carrie rolled onto her stomach, jugulars bulging as she screeched. She dragged herself through the neighboring archway and entered the kitchen. Her cell phone was on the counter next to a tray of uncooked chicken breasts and other ingredients. She didn't have a plan to reach it, she just knew she *needed* it to survive.

Micah followed her trail of blood. In the kitchen, just a few feet away from the counters, he bent forward over her and smiled. He was amused by her will to live. *So old yet so desperate,* he thought. He held the hunting knife in the icepick grip, then he stabbed her with a rapid succession of thrusts. He stabbed her across the upper back, riddling her with holes from shoulder to shoulder. Then he stabbed her towards the center of her back four times.

The apron's strap was cut. Blood pooled underneath her, flowing down the grooves between the kitchen tiles. She tried to use it to her advantage, but she couldn't slide away.

"*Ahh! Ah… Ahh!*" Carrie screamed through the stabbing. "He… Help! Help me! Fish–Fisher!"

She stopped screaming as Micah thrust the blade into her lower back. He snapped her lumbar spine. He twisted the blade inside of her, listening to the muffled *crunch* of her bones. Her legs stopped shaking. She slowly lowered her head until her chin rested on a bloody tile. She stared at a kitchen cabinet while gasping for air. Then, unable to handle the pain, she fell unconscious.

"Sleep, baby, sleep," Micah said. "We'll finish our little date later."

He looked through his backpack. He used a zip-tie handcuff to restrain her arms behind her back at the wrists. He slapped a strip of duct tape over her mouth. He figured it was enough to stop her from escaping or screaming. He peered out the kitchen window. He saw a boy riding his bike in circles on the street. He didn't notice anything out of the ordinary.

Micah went into the living room. The framed photographs on the fireplace mantle caught his eye. It showed an older Asian man—Phillip Fei, Fisher's father—dressed in hunting attire with a rifle in his hands posing with other men. At the center of each picture, there was a dead animal—a hunting trophy. He posed with a black wildebeest, a bushpig, and a black bear. His trophy hunting led him across the globe, gunning down animals for sport and pleasure.

Micah couldn't blame him. He loved hunting people, especially women, through the concrete jungle. The thrill of the hunt was unparalleled.

"You're a killer in disguise, aren't you?" Micah said as he tapped one of the pictures.

He looked outside through the glass sliding doors. The backyard was clean, grassed trimmed and furniture dusted, but it was vacant. He went down the hall. The first door to the left led to a bathroom. Again, it was clean but empty. The first door to the right led to a home office. He spotted more pictures of Phillip's hunting adventures. He went across the hall to the second door to the left.

He stood in the doorway, impressed. It was a tiny laundry room. The hamper, the laundry machines, and the water heater were to the left. To the right, there was a cabinet with cleaning supplies and home improvement tools. Beyond that cabinet, a tall, heavy-duty steel rifle safe was bolted to the ground. It required a six-digit code.

1-2-3-4-5-6.

Micah turned the handle, but it didn't open. He whispered, "I'll be back for you..."

He approached the door across the hall. He pushed it open and peeked into the room. A high-definition television sat on a six-drawer dresser to the left. The closet at the other end of the room was closed, the floor around the door littered with dirty socks and t-shirts. To the right, there was a loft bed. Under the elevated bed, there was a desk with a computer.

Fisher Fei sat at the desk, wearing a pair of noise-cancelling headphones while playing Fortnite on his computer. He was a short, scrawny Chinese American guy. At twenty-nine years old, his wispy hair was already thinning. His dark brown eyes told stories of loneliness and nihilism. Pitted acne scars dug tiny craters into his perpetually rosy cheeks.

Micah was shocked by his discovery. The man in the bedroom—that short, feeble, gaunt man—was responsible for his transformation. Fisher had manipulated him, spinning tall tales of his own good looks and spitting war stories of his violent experiences on the frontlines of the incel movement. But that man in the room wasn't a lady's man and he looked like he couldn't hurt a fly.

Arguing with another player, Fisher said, "You're a fucking faggot, bro. No, shut up... Fuck off... Seriously, fuck off, you simp. Kill yourself."

Fisher couldn't hear his mother's suffering due to the headphones. He was sucked into the online world of video games and trolling. Micah took the pistol out of his backpack. He aimed it at Fisher's torso as he sidestepped towards the loft bed. Fisher saw him from the corner of his eye. He thought it was his mother at first, then he noticed the gun.

"Holy shit," he said as he took off his headphones. He kicked the desk and pushed himself away on the rolling chair. He put his hands up and begged, "Don't shoot. Holy shit, man, please don't shoot."

"Don't you... Wait, don't you recognize me?"

"Wha–What?" Fisher stuttered. He lowered his head while keeping his hands in the air. He said, "No... N–No, man, I didn't see your face. Take whatever you want and leave."

"You don't recognize me because I never showed you my face," Micah whispered. His smile said something like: *I'll be damned.* He demanded, "Look at me, Fisher."

"N–No..."

Micah bent over and pointed the gun at Fisher's face. He repeated, "Look at me, Fisher."

"No, man, please. I–I don't want to see you. You just take it, take it all, a–and go. I won't tell the police anything, I swear."

"Look at me, *Fish.*"

Fish—the word was common, people spoke about fish every day, but there was no reason for an intruder to call him Fish. He only used that username on the Fuck-Less forums. Anyone could connect his home address to his real name with an online search. But only one person could connect his username to his home address. He raised his head slowly until he stared down the barrel of the gun. He gazed into Micah's zany eyes.

He said, "You... Are you..."

"TaxiDriver94," Micah said. "Micah Watson. You remember me, don't you? You're not going to act stupid again, are you?"

Fisher could only nod as memories raced through his mind. He thought about every conversation he ever shared with Micah. *When did I tell him my address?*—he thought. He glanced at the door. He heard a muffled whimper. It could have been a mouse in the walls or a kid outside, but he knew it was his mother.

Voice shaking, he asked, "Did you hurt my mom?"

"We'll get to that later."

"He–Hey, she has n–nothing to do with this. I was just–"

"Fisher, I need you to stop talking about your 'mommy,' okay?" Micah interrupted. He leaned back against the wall behind him, the gun aimed at Fisher's torso. He said, "Something's not right, is it? I'm standing here in your parents' house, watching you play video games under a bunk bed, as skinny as a skeleton, as short as a child in middle school... You said you were an executive at some billion-dollar company, you had girlfriends in the past, you *weren't* a virgin, you were a guru on men's freedom and masculinity. You said you were a 'player,' but I didn't think you were talking about fucking video games! You owe me a damn explanation, Fisher. Who are you?"

"Wha–What do you mean? Like... what the hell do you mean, man?"

"I don't know. I really don't know. Why don't you start by telling me about yourself, hmm?"

Fisher's eyes darted to the door again. He heard another muffled whimper. His face scrunched, then he bit his lip and shook his head. He had to fight to stop himself from breaking down.

He asked, "Can you at least tell me if my mom's okay?"

"She's fine. I knocked her down, then I tied her up, but she'll live. Now, *drop it.* Answer my question before I go out there and shove this gun into your mom's ass and shoot a bullet through the top of her skull."

"Oh s–shit," Fisher whimpered. He took a deep breath, then he said, "Okay, okay. My name is... My name is Fisher Fei. I'm, uh... I'm twenty-nine years old. I–I think I told you that before... Um... I don't have a job. I used to work as a janitor, but I quit because I thought it was holding me back. That was a... a mistake. And, um... I guess... Yeah, I'm an incel. I just... I lied about having a girlfriend. I've never dated anyone before. I've never even been close to dating someone. Never kissed anyone, never held a girl's hand, never... I never even hugged a girl, even when I was a young kid. I was the boy that didn't get a Valentine's Day card in elementary school. You know, those days when everyone is supposed to get a card? I was that *one* kid who didn't get a thing."

Micah saw a part of himself in Fisher. They shared similar lives filled with loneliness and neglect. As a matter of fact, he could have replaced his life with Fisher's and it would have been pretty much the same. But he didn't feel any sympathy for him.

He said, "You said you killed people before."

"I–I didn't."

"You did. You said there were only two ways to know if you were blackpilled: by fucking a hooker or hurting women."

"But–But I never said I hurt anyone."

"But you made it sound like you did! Was it all lies? Have you ever killed anyone before? Huh? Answer me, you cuck!"

Fisher lowered his head in shame. The chair made a *squeaky* sound as he trembled on it.

He said, "No… I've never killed anyone. I told you to do it because… I don't know, man. I was… I guess I wanted to live through you. Every time you came home and told me about what you did, every time I read about you on the news, I felt like *I* was doing it, too. Finally, people were scared of me. People noticed me… *You,* I mean, they noticed you. Then I got scared. I read about people getting arrested for encouraging others to break the law. I didn't need to put my finger on a trigger to get arrested for murder. So, you were right: I pussied out. I had to stop or you'd take us both down. That's it. That's my story."

Micah said, "That's not the whole story. Tell me something, Fisher. Why did you become an incel? You always told me shit like 'girls cheat' or 'Mackenzie's probably fucking other guys.' But you just said you never dated anyone. Are you really part of this 'movement?' Or are you just a troll?"

Fisher said, "Micah, I... I'm an incel. I never dated anyone, but that doesn't mean I didn't try. When I was in college, I fell in love with this girl. Her name was Jessica. She was Chinese... a foreign-exchange student. She was nice to me. She made me feel good about myself. We spent months talking, you know, just like you and Mackenzie... But when I asked her out, she told me she was already dating someone. She was dating a white guy. That might mean nothing to you, but for me..." Fisher swallowed loudly as tears were flicked off his eyelashes with each blink. He said, "Think of it this way: how would you feel if every woman in your race rejected you for men of other races? If they treated you like an ugly, disgusting creature while *worshipping* other men? Because that's exactly what Asian women do. They reject safe, nice guys like me and they'll fall head over fucking heels for the ugliest white guy who looks their way! That's why I became a fucking incel, Micah! Because my own people—my own women—hate me! Okay?!"

A dead silence befell the room. The men gazed at each other for a minute. Then another muffled groaned broke the silence.

Micah smiled at him and asked, "Now why didn't you use that anger and take matters into your own hands? Why didn't you take one of daddy's guns and shoot up a country concert?"

"Be–Because... I'm weak. I'm a–a pussy. Incels... We're not really violent people. We troll a lot and sometimes we lose control of ourselves, but we're not out there killing people every day. We have violent thoughts, but we don't act on them. You... You, Micah, you're the violent type. We're just trying to make things fair while having some fun. But you're our loudspeaker. And that's that. Can I please see my mom now?"

Micah's eyes wandered in every direction—left, right, up, down. He sniffled and swiped at his nose. He was hurt by Fisher's manipulative behavior. He was reminded of Mackenzie. He believed they used him, then they threw him aside like garbage when they were done. They were the same. Every single person on the planet was the same.

Selfish.

Manipulative.

Self-destructive.

He trusted himself to fix the world. *A human genocide,* he thought, *no discrimination, just a modern cleansing.*

He said, "Fisher, is your dad home?"

"He... He's on a business trip. You can't hurt him... can't kill him."

"Well, that's a good and a bad thing. It's bad because, as you know, I can't kill him. And it's good because... now no one can stop me from killing your precious mother."

"Wha–What? Wa–Wait, Micah, pl–please don–"

Micah lunged forward and grabbed Fisher's hair. He pulled him off the chair and dragged him out of the bedroom. Fisher swung at him, hitting his forearm, his back, and his abs, but his fists couldn't hurt him. He had bones like a baby's. He injured his own hands more than he hurt Micah.

Micah pushed him into the kitchen through an archway. They found Carrie on the floor, about an inch away from the counters. She had regained consciousness, but she barely moved a couple of inches. She cried as she spotted her son.

"Mom!" Fisher cried.

Micah grabbed the back of his shirt and stopped him from running to his mother's side. He pushed Fisher to the floor, forcing him to sit on his ass in front of the refrigerator.

He pressed the gun against the side of his head and said, "You move, she dies."

"Please, please, please," Fisher begged, speaking quickly. "Don't kill us. I was just fucking around, man. Please! Please, Micah! *Fuck!*"

As his former friend begged for mercy, Micah tucked the pistol into the back of his waistband. He grabbed the roll of duct tape from his backpack. He taped Fisher's right arm to the cabinet beside the refrigerator—ten strips of tape over his wrist, another ten over his forearm, and five more over the crook of his elbow. The cabinet door was just a decoration, so it couldn't be opened. It was enough to stop Fisher from moving.

As he scratched the tape, trying to peel it off, Fisher cried, "Don't! I'm sorry! I'm so–"

"Don't touch that tape, you rat! If you take even one piece of it off, if I see you trying to stand up, I'm going to kill this bitch! You hear me?!"

"Goddammit, Micah! Please!"

Fisher was scared and frustrated, but he followed Micah's directions. He couldn't break free without alarming Micah and he couldn't overpower him in a fair fight anyway. Micah stepped over Carrie. He huffed upon hearing her weak, trembling voice behind the tape on her mouth. It sounded like she was trying to pray. Micah grabbed a rolling pin from the counter.

The handles of the rolling pin were about three inches long. At its widest point, the rolling pin's handles had a circumference of five and a half inches.

Micah crouched beside Carrie's legs. He said, "Fisher, I need you to tell me the passcode to your dad's rifle safe. If you don't help me, I will have to hurt your mom. As you can see, she's already out for the count. I broke her spine, but I'm pretty sure she'll still feel what I have planned for her. Help your mother and help your old friend. What do you say?"

Fisher's mind was overwhelmed with horrifying questions: *what's he going to do with that? If I give him the passcode, he'll just kill us with my dad's guns, right? Are we trapped? Is there really no way out of this?* He didn't care if Micah used the guns to shoot up an elementary school. He only cared about his own survival. His heart told him to negotiate.

He stuttered, "I–I'll tell you. Just take my mom to the living room and... and put something on her cuts to–to stop the bleeding. Then... Then call 911 and–"

"Wrong answer, friend."

Micah pushed Carrie's dress up. He chuckled at her flabby ass and high-waisted underwear. *Sunny's was better,* he thought. He pulled her underwear down to her knees. Carrie felt her underwear sliding away from her waist, but she couldn't move her legs.

Fisher yelled, "Stop! Fucking asshole! Leave her alone!"

Micah ignored him. He spread her ass and took a gander at her genitals. He snickered as he saw her dry labia. He wasn't expecting her to be aroused, but it looked ashen to him—*dusty.* He had only ever seen Sunny's vagina in person, though. Her anus was tight. He rubbed one of the rolling pin's rough handles around her anus, ringing it like a vulture circling its prey.

Carrie whine as she moved her shoulders from side to side, moving away from Micah at a snail's pace. Then she closed her eyes and held her breath, head shaking uncontrollably. Fisher gasped and looked away, horrified. Micah had penetrated Carrie's anus with the rolling pin, forcing all three inches of the handle into her ass.

"How does that feel, bitch?" Micah asked. "Big enough for ya?"

He pulled it two inches out, then he thrust it into her again. He twisted it inside of her. He pulled it out two inches and repeated the process. He fucked her with the rolling pin's handle. Despite her broken spine, a burning pain roared across her pelvis. She felt like she was being impaled, like a football was being shoved up her anus, like her rectal walls were being dragged out of her.

Blood stained the handle after a couple of thrusts. Splinters from the handle tore into her rectum. A drop of blood rolled down to her vagina.

Carrie unleashed a muffled shriek. It barely escaped the house, dying on the front lawn before it could reach any of their neighbors. Sobbing uncontrollably, Fisher mumbled the same word over and over: *no, no, no, no, no!* He was an incel, he grew to hate women from all backgrounds, but he always loved his mother.

The handle came out of Carrie's anus with a *plopping* sound. Her genitals were covered in blood. Her rectum had prolapsed, squeezed out of her anus and resembling the pistil of a flower.

Over the hysterical weeping, Micah said, "Fisher, tell me the passcode. End her suffering before I get more ideas."

Fisher cried, "No, God. No, no, no…"

"What else can I do to her? I can stick a wire hanger up her pussy and scrape her insides out. How does that sound?"

"Holy shit, no…"

"I can cut her titties off and tape 'em to your head. I can pull her teeth out, *one*-by-*one*, then throat-fuck her until she suffocates. I can chew on her clitoris, like gum. Chew on it until it's just mush. Or you can tell me the passcode. What's it going to be?"

Tell him!—Carrie tried to yell it out, but it was unintelligible. Yet, Fisher knew exactly what she was trying to say. He glanced at Micah, then he looked straight ahead. He didn't want to see his mother in that position.

"Oh my God," Fisher whined.

"*Oh my God, Becky,*" Micah said mockingly in a shrill voice. He said, "Fine. I'll make it quicker for us. If you don't give me the passcode in ten seconds, I'm going to bash her skull in with this rolling pin. Ten, nine, eight, seven, six..."

"Fucking asshole. I hate you, you fucking..."

"Five, four..."

"Oh fuck. Fuck!"

"Three, two..."

"Okay! I'll tell you!" Fisher yelled. He dropped his head and said, "It's sixty-five, sixty-eight, ninety-one."

"Six-five-six-eight-nine-one?"

Fisher nodded. Micah glared at him, trying to decipher the sincerity behind his words. Carrie kept groaning, barely awake.

Micah said, "I'll be right back. Remember: you move, she dies."

He rushed out of the kitchen and made his way to the laundry room. He punched the passcode into the rifle safe's keypad: *656891*. He heard a loud *click*. He turned the handle and pulled the door open. He couldn't stop himself from grinning as he admired the small armory. He returned to the kitchen and threw the rolling pin into the sink.

He said, "You didn't lie to me. I appreciate that. So, I'm not going to cave her head in with that rolling pin? You wanna know why?"

Fish mumbled incoherently, like a boy scolded by his mother in a shopping mall.

Micah explained, "Because we need to add some variety to this show. Because I'm going to cave her fucking head in with this frying pan instead."

He grabbed a heavy skillet from the stove.

Fisher finally looked at him and yelled, "No!"

But it was too late. A word couldn't stop Micah anyway. Micah swung the skillet at the back of Carrie's head. Her scalp was split open instantly. Her face hit the tile floor with so much force that her nose and cheekbones shattered like glass. She felt a stinging pain in her skull. The blood running across her scalp was boiling, like fresh soup. She moaned loudly.

Micah struck her head again. He heard her scalp *shredding* with the blow, tearing like paper. Through her bloody, tangled hair and the fleshy, wide gash, he could see a slit of her skull. With each hit, a *clunk* and a *clang* echoed through the house. The back of her skull cracked after the eighth blow. After a minute, her skull was caved in. Bits of her crushed brain oozed out, prolapsing from her head like her anus.

After three minutes of nonstop pounding, the top of her skull was detached. Her hair floated in a puddle of blood underneath her, swimming with fragments of her skull and chunks of her brain. The dented body of the skillet snapped off the handle. It hit the wall, then it landed on the floor in front of Fisher.

Micah threw the handle at the sink. He placed his hands on his hips and caught his breath as he stared down at Carrie's crushed head. It reminded him of Samantha Brown's face after he ran her head over with his car. He was desensitized to the violence. He stepped over her and approached Fisher. He watched him as he cowered and cried.

He said, "You hurt me. You were supposed to be my friend, but you... you betrayed me. And you know what? I wouldn't have done any of this if you just answered your messages. If you gave me your dad's guns, I wouldn't have cared what you looked like. But you *betrayed* me, Fisher. You're the worst type of incel—the spineless type." He drew his hunting knife and said, "Now let's make you dick-less, too."

Wide-eyed, Fish yelled, "What?! No! No, Micah! Oh my God, please!"

Micah pulled Fisher's shorts down. His flaccid penis looked like a bean hidden in a wiry bush of pubic hair.

Fisher screamed, "Help me! Somebody help me!"

His shouts reached the street, but no one was around to hear him. Micah grabbed the glans of his penis and stretched it away from his crotch. Fisher clawed at Micah's forearm with his free hand, he kicked and moved his hips, but to no avail. With a single swipe of the long blade, Micah severed his penis near the base—and he trimmed some of his pubic hairs, too.

He chuckled as he threw it at Fisher's face. It stained his nose with blood, then fell onto his shirt. Blood shot out of his crotch in squirts, like piss after sex. The pain—the hot, thrumming pain—shot through his pelvis, then ran up his spine and flowed down his legs. His heartbeat accelerated while his brain thumped. His eyes nearly popped out of their sockets. His screaming became louder, hitting the houses next door and even the house across the street.

Micah took another zip-tie out of his backpack. While Fisher was distracted by the pain, he slid the zip-tie over Fisher's head, then he tightened it around his neck. Fisher's scream transformed into a loud gurgle. He scratched his neck, then he slapped his palm over his mutilated crotch, then he scratched his neck again. He wanted to break the zip-tie while placing pressure on his wound. He tried to break free from the tape, but he was weaker than ever.

His eyes began to roll back. The color faded from his lips. His cheeks went from blushed to ashen and then bluish. He hopped on his ass, trying to stand up, but he couldn't because of his taped arm.

Micah crouched in front of him and said, "Fisher Fei, my friend, you're flopping like a... like a *fish* out of water."

Then the sides of his mouth fell. A croaking sound came out of Fisher's gaping mouth. It was slow and awful—almost demonic. Fisher suffocated after three minutes, eyes rolled back and eyelids open. The croaking sound continued for fifteen seconds afterward. And Micah heard it for another minute as he watched Fisher's dead body with a look of disappointment.

He felt like a frog was stuck in his skull, croaking and ribbiting endlessly.

Micah said, "Sweet dreams, Fisher."

He went to the laundry room. The rifle safe was loaded with a shotgun, a bolt-action centerfire rifle, and a semi-automatic rifle. He thought about taking all of the guns, but he couldn't carry everything. So, he took the AR-15. It was customized with a bump stock to simulate automatic fire and a high-capacity magazine holding one hundred rounds.

He said, "You're a beaut, aren't ya?"

He carefully placed the rifle in his bag. He opened a small drawer inside the safe. He found two holstered handguns—one semi-automatic pistol, one revolver. He stuffed all three into his backpack. He grabbed three magazines for the pistol, too. He zipped up his backpack, but the barrel of the rifle protruded out of it. It didn't bother him at all.

He walked past the kitchen archways. He saw Fisher, back against the refrigerator, head slumped down, arm taped to the cabinet. Then he saw Carrie, ass covered in blood and head crushed to bits. It was a bloodbath. He exited the house, strolling down the walkway to the front gate with a bag full of guns. The neighbors didn't notice. As he drove away in his car, he honked and waved at the boy riding his bike on the street.

The kid waved back at him, unaware of Micah's monstrous actions.

Micah whispered, "I'm doing this for you, kid. It's time for the next step."

Chapter Eighteen

The Nail Salon

Micah cruised past an insurance office, a laundromat, and a sushi restaurant before spotting Lee's Nails. Through the storefront windows, he could see the salon was full of women of all ages and races. He spotted a young teenager—fourteen, maybe fifteen years old. He saw her laughing, but he felt like he could hear her, too. He couldn't wait to wipe the joy off her face.

The location was perfect. His targets were seated on large, comfy chairs. Some soaked their feet in warm baths, others waited for their nails to dry. A couple of women stood around the chairs, chatting with their friends. A few ladies sat in the waiting area, lined up in front of the storefront windows. There were two flamboyant men inside the salon, gossiping with the girls, as well as an average Joe.

Micah took a left in front of Lee's Nails. The parking lot was full because of the private party, so he had to park at the other end of the lot—about thirty meters away from the shop. He stopped the car.

Gazing at his reflection on the rear-view mirror, he said, "This is your time, Micah. They're in there, laughing and gossiping and mocking us. You go in there and you show them that this is *still* a man's world. Wipe them out and set an example. Send the signal and... and start a real sex war. You can do this. Let's do it! Come on!"

He reached into the backseat and grabbed a large, heavy duffel bag. He threw the bag on the passenger seat—*clunk!* It was full of his armor. He already wore the Kevlar vest under his coveralls. He strapped the steel kneepads to his knees and the shoulder pads to his shoulders. Then he strapped the chest plate to his chest.

He reclined his seat and leaned forward. He slid the back plate between himself and the seat, then he leaned back against it. He connected the back plate to the chest plate, then he tightened the straps. He ran his fingers through his sweaty hair, then he wiped his gloved hands on his thighs. Despite being drenched in sweat, he put on his helmet.

The weather was pleasant—warm with a cool breeze—but he felt like he was sitting in an oven, filling his lungs with hot air and smoke. He was roasting inside of his car, sweat soaking every inch of his body. Sopping locks of his hair stuck out from under the helmet. He slapped his neck as a bead of sweat tickled his skin. He rolled the window down an inch.

"Don't lose your cool, Micah," he told himself. He looked at the dashboard clock: *6:12 PM.* He said, "Just a few more minutes, then you have to move, okay?"

He checked his weapons. The HK P30L pistol was loaded with a ten-round magazine. He checked the revolver's cylinder—six cartridges. The other pistol, a Glock 17, had another ten-round magazine. He holstered the HK P30L while tucking the other handguns behind his belt. He glanced around as he checked the AR15. It was more conspicuous than the other guns. *Locked and loaded,* he thought.

He sat and watched the nail salon from afar. He ducked whenever a customer from one of the neighboring stores walked past his car. He kept his eyes peeled for any police officers or mall security guards, too. He wanted to confirm Mackenzie's presence in the shop before starting his assault. He couldn't identify anyone from his position, though.

Two women departed from the shop, one woman arrived to a mocking applause—*late, again*. The herd was thinning.

Breathing heavily, Micah said, "There's no turning back. You killed Fisher and his mom. You didn't clean the crime scene. This is the end. Don't let it fizzle out. This isn't the conclusion they asked for. End it with a bang... Send the signal... Now or never." He slapped himself twice, then he yelled, "Do it, Micah! Show them who's boss!"

6:45 PM.

Rifle in hand, Micah exited his car. He didn't close the door behind him. He felt like he was moving in slow motion as he walked around his car, his armor shuffling with each step.

The sun fell beyond the strip mall, casting golden rays of sunshine onto the parking lot. Vehicles zoomed down the street in front of the mall. Others waited at the red light, eager to race to their destinations. An older, middle-aged woman pushed a cart of groceries to a minivan, her seven-year-old daughter skipping behind her. There were no cops or security guards in sight.

Micah marched towards the salon—twenty-five meters, twenty meters, fifteen meters, ten meters. He stopped on the street, just ten meters away from the shop. He could see his reflection on the storefront window. It was business as usual inside of Lee's Nails. The chatter was loud and the cackling obnoxious. They didn't notice the armed and armored man watching them from outside.

Do it, do it, do it, do it, do it, Micah's inner voice repeated.

He aimed the rifle at the shop and placed his finger on the trigger. He scanned the women, searching for Mackenzie in the group. While doing so, a woman spotted him as she exited the sushi place next door. She gasped, then she ran back into the restaurant.

"Oh my God, he has a gun!" her voice escaped the restaurant before the door closed behind her.

Micah squeezed the trigger. The rifle screamed. Each round *cracked* and *thumped.* The storefront windows shattered in less than a second after he pulled the trigger. He fired in bursts to control the recoil and conserve ammunition. He heard ringing in his ears, but he welcomed it. He was tired of hearing women anyway.

A young woman, Monica, sitting in the seating area was shot in the back of her head. The bullet burst out through her right eye. Gooey strands from Monica's ruptured eye, along with bits of her brain, hung over her cheek. She fell forward, slid off her seat, and hit the floor face first, blood erupting from the wound at the back of her head.

One dead.

The through-and-through round also struck another woman, Karla, at one of the salon chairs. The bullet shattered her right ankle. The water in the foot bath turned red. She leapt off the chair, howling in pain. At the seating area, Tiffany was shot in the shoulder. The bullet pushed her broken clavicle *out* through the gaping exit wound on her chest. She curled into the fetal position on the chair, shrieking.

Shards of glass rained down on the seating areas, slicing the women. The other bullets from the first burst hit the floor and furniture.

Micah took a step forward and shot at the shop again. A bullet went through her chair and hit Tiffany's lower back. She crawled onto the woman beside her, Emily. Emily sat with her palms over her ears, eyes closed, and head down, screaming in horror. The other women in the seating area hit the floor with their fingers laced over the backs of their heads.

Two bullets struck Linda, one of the salon employees. The first round went through her rib cage, burrowing through both of her lungs. The other went through her pelvis, breaking her bones and stopping in her uterus. She tried to run to the back of the store as soon as she felt the sharp burning pain, but she collapsed after a few steps. She gasped for air, but her lungs were flooded with blood.

At another chair, Daniela, another customer, was shot through the throat before she could stand up. She fell back into the chair and gripped her neck with both hands. Her feet slid in the foot bath as she convulsed on the chair. A salon employee, Judy, grabbed Daniela's arms and tried to pull her off the seat. Three bullets riddled Judy's chest, puncturing her heart and collapsing a lung. She collapsed on top of Daniela, trapping her on the chair. Daniela suffocated—slowly and painfully.

Two dead.

Three dead.

Micah couldn't hear the wheels screeching on the street or the customers screaming in the other stores. He focused only on the nail salon. He shot at the shop again. The third burst of gunfire missed his targets. Bullets struck the mirrors, the chairs, and the walls. He stepped forward and adjusted his aim. He shot at them a fourth time.

Jamie, another salon employee, was shot while dragging Linda behind a chair. The bullet entered the top of her head and exited through the nape of her neck. She collapsed on top of Linda, dead in an instant.

Four dead.

Linda whined and coughed as bullets whizzed past her, hitting the furniture and the customers. Face against the floor, she couldn't push Jamie off of her. She tried to yell—*help!*—but only a croak came out. She turned pale and cold. She thought about her daughters as she choked on her own blood. She wanted to hold them again.

Five dead.

Two employees, Nora and Cecil, were shot in the back as they went into the back office. Nora was hit in the thigh and lower back while Cecil was shot through the ribcage. They fell to the floor and scrambled under a desk. Some of the customers followed their lead, running into the office with their heads down. One woman crawled into the office on all fours, slipping and sliding on her friends' blood.

Jose activated the storefront gate with a key and a button on the wall near the reception desk. He hoped to save as many lives as possible by adding a layer of protection between them and the shooter—a shield. The gate rattled as it descended slowly. It barely reached the top of the door before Micah shot him.

Jose was hit in the chest four times and once in the chin. The last bullet split his jaw open vertically down the center. His mutilated tongue hung out of the massive opening. He fell back over the desk behind him.

Six dead.

Micah ran up to the entrance. He leaned into the store through the shattered storefront windows. He found Emily and Tiffany, along with three other women, laying on the floor on their stomachs. They were surrounded by glass and blood—so much glass and blood.

Emily yelled, "Oh my God! Please! I don't–"

Micah aimed the rifle down at them and fired. He couldn't help but smile. He felt like Tony Montana at the end of Scarface—confident, powerful, *unstoppable*. The actual ending of the movie didn't cross his mind, so he didn't pay attention to his surroundings.

Emily's back was riddled with bullets. She let out one last bellow before dying. Tiffany tried to squeeze herself under Emily to use her as a human shield. It was an awful thing to do, but survival was the only thing on her mind. She couldn't escape Micah's rage. He shot the small of her back four times and her ass three times.

Seven dead.

Eight dead.

Two of the other women scrambled towards the back. One of them was killed instantly with a bullet to the head. The other young lady was shot through her upper back four times. She hit the floor face first and glided across the tiles, like a child on a water slide.

Nine dead.

Ten dead.

The last woman, Michelle, suffered the worst fate. She ran towards the entrance, hoping to sprint past the shooter, but she was shot once in the shoulder. She fell back like a falling tree. Her scream came to a halt as she hit the floor beside Emily and Tiffany. The air was knocked out of her. She rocked side to side.

"No, no, God, no," she mewled. Micah aimed at her. She cried, "I don't wanna die. Pl–Please, don't ki–"

Micah squeezed the trigger. He shot her head twelve times. Each bullet tore a chunk of skin off her face, practically flaying her. Her cheeks and forehead were torn off, leaving mushy flesh and broken bone behind. The top of her skull—the crown—was blown off her head. A massive lump of her brain spilled out. Her teeth were visible through a hole on the side of her face while the same bullet severed her ear. Her jaw was dislocated and broken. Her head was reduced to bloody pulp.

Eleven dead.

Micah pushed the door open and peeked inside. The walls were decorated with bullet holes and streaks of blood. Shards of glass swam in the puddles of blood on the floor. Dust floated in the air. Some of the lights flickered, others were shot out. He heard women crying and whining from every direction. It was music to his ears—the soundtrack to his perfect world. He narrowed his eyes and smirked upon spotting a woman crouching behind a salon chair—*Beverly Bennet.*

She was barefoot and covered in blood, but she wasn't injured. She tried to stop a friend from bleeding out, but she couldn't save the dead.

"Bev," Micah whispered.

He aimed the rifle at her. He squeezed the trigger—*nothing.* To his dismay, the magazine was empty. He threw the rifle aside and quickly drew his HK P30L. He shot at Bev as she made a run for the back office. He shot a mirror, a chair, another mirror, a wall, then he hit her. She yelped and she kept lurching away.

He squinted down the sights, following her with the pistol. Explosive gunfire echoed through the streets—but it didn't come from Micah's gun. A police officer shot at him from the parking lot. A bullet hit Micah's shoulder pad with enough force to make him stagger. Two bullets hit his back plate as he stumbled away.

Micah shot back at the cop. He hit the pavement and a car. The cop ran backwards to redeploy. He let off another shot, hitting Micah in the hip. Micah screamed as he fell. He pushed himself up to his feet, then he fell again. From the pavement, he shot at the cop—one, two, three times. He hit the cop's kneecap with the third shot, causing him to collapse.

Micah seized the opportunity and launched himself up to his feet. He limped behind an SUV. He heard another gunshot. He heard emergency sirens, too. He was out of time. He threw the pistol aside. He knew the magazine was empty. He drew the Glock 17 instead. He drew a deep, shaky breath, then he leaned out from behind the SUV and shot at the cop. The officer fired back while calling for reinforcements.

Micah hid behind the SUV again, wincing as bullets broke the window and ricocheted off the steel. As the gunfire stopped, he leaned out and shot at the cop again. He hit the cop's chest twice. Both rounds penetrated his ballistic vest. His pistol fell out of his hand and the back of his head hit the pavement. He stared at the sky, bloody mist spraying out of his mouth with each cough.

"He's a goner," Micah said as he listened to the cop's suffering.

He limped over to his car. The sirens grew louder as the cops and paramedics approached. He climbed into his car and took off his helmet. He swiped his fingers through his hair, inadvertently turning some of his frosted tips red with his blood. He rubbed his hair with his other hand, but he just spread more of his blood across his scalp.

He chuckled in disbelief. He placed the pistol on the passenger seat and drove away. He wanted to avoid the cops, but he was ready to shoot them from his car if it came down to that.

One hand over his wound and the other on the steering wheel, he said, "Good... I'm good. I'm still alive and I... I have enough ammo to kill that bitch... to kill anyone who gets in my way. I'm just like–" He hissed in pain as the car rocked. He took a right and drove out of the parking lot. Teary-eyed, face tight as he fought the urge to cry, he said, "I'm just like the Supreme Gentleman. He'd be proud of me. Fisher, too. I'm a martyr. A hero. I'll be all over... all over the news. It's almost over. One more stop. One more..."

Chapter Nineteen

The Grand Finale

The dashboard clock read: *6:58 PM*.

In less than nine minutes, Micah killed more than ten people, including a cop, and he injured many more. He had been driving for about four minutes, swerving in and out of traffic while trying to control his bleeding. A tingly sensation accompanied the *burn* of the gunshot. It spread across his pelvic region. Blood soaked his leg and the driver's seat. He felt himself sitting on his hot blood.

The other drivers honked at him and stomped on their brakes, barely avoiding head-on collisions. Emergency sirens and flashing lights followed his trail.

"You're almost there, Micah," he muttered. He placed more pressure on the gas pedal. He said, "Don't give up yet. Kill this bitch and change the world. Kill her! Kill them all!"

He zoomed past a red light. He drove past small bars and cafés. He stomped on his brakes upon spotting a bright red sign—*Mario's Diner, Open 24 Hours*. The car skidded to a stop in front of the diner. The news was just beginning to spread. It reached the city's residents through Twitter and Facebook first. The headlines went something like this: *Potential active shooter at Pinecreek Strip Mall.*

Some of the patrons and employees at Mario's Diner were aware of the shooting, but they were nearly a mile away from the scene. They didn't see a reason to evacuate or barricade themselves in the restaurant. As far as they knew, a worker was going postal at the mall. They weren't concerned with violence until it touched *their* lives.

Micah stumbled out of the car, pants leg soaked in blood. Pistol in hand, he limped to the diner. The door chime rang through the restaurant as he pushed the door open.

Sandra Madrid approached the entrance. She said, "How many are we sitting today?"

She gasped and stepped back upon noticing Micah's armor, his sweat, his tears, and his blood. Then she saw the pistol in his hand. She raised her hands to her chest, a pen in one hand and an order pad in the other.

She stuttered, "Don–Don't shoot. I'm just a–"

Micah locked the door behind him. He poked Sandra's shoulder with the pistol, causing her to wince and teeter back.

He said, "Don't move or I'll blow your fucking brains out." He looked at the kitchen over the bar and shouted, "Mackenzie! I know you're here! I know your shift just started! Mackenzie, get your ass out here! Get out here *right now* or your friend dies!"

"Oh my God, please don't kill me," Sandra begged. A stream of urine ran down her leg, soaking her work pants. She said, "I–I'm only twenty. I'm a–a kid."

"He has a gun," a man whispered from a booth in the corner.

In a booth at the opposite corner, another man said, "Put your heads down. Don't look. It's okay, just don't look." He was trying to comfort his young son and daughter.

His wife whimpered, "Oh God, oh no."

Micah yelled, "*Get out here!*"

An elderly man at the bar folded his newspaper and stood from his stool with his hands up. He said, "Now, let's calm down here, young man. You don't want to do this. Let's–"

"Shut. The. Fuck. *Up!*" Micah ordered as he pointed the gun at him. The man sat down and mumbled something. As she took another step back, Micah aimed the pistol at Sandra again. He said, "Move again, bitch. I dare you."

Sandra clasped her hands and apologized in a jumble of incoherent words, tears cascading down her cheeks like waterfalls. The man stood from his booth, one arm outstretched to protect his family. Two cooks ran through the kitchen and headed to the exit at the back of the diner. One cook stayed in front of the fryers. He had an opportunity to escape, but fear had a funny way of paralyzing people. Another waitress stood near a table with a young couple, a coffee pot in her hand—the coffee *sloshing* as she trembled uncontrollably.

Mario Chavez came out of the break room behind the counter with his hands up. He shuddered, although he tried to look calm.

Micah said, "No, not you. I want to see…"

He stopped as Mackenzie emerged from the break room with her hands up. Another waitress hid under the table in the back, too scared to move. Eyes glistening with tears, Mackenzie cocked her head to the side upon spotting Micah. She hadn't recognized his voice—it was deeper and meaner—but she couldn't forget his face or frosted tips. She couldn't believe it. The shy, awkward young man she once befriended at that very same diner had turned into a cold-blooded killer.

Micah smirked and said, "There's my Big Mac. God, I've been waiting so long for this day. How are you doing?"

Mackenzie stuttered, "Mi–Mi–Micah, wha–what are–"

Micah squeezed the trigger and shot Sandra in the head. A streak of blood and bits of her brain exploded from the hole at the back of her skull. She folded over herself, as if she were shot in the stomach, and she collapsed next to a booth with a cowering elderly couple. The patrons screamed and sobbed, ducking under their tables and dashing towards the kitchen.

A burly man rushed Micah from one of the booths. Micah leaned to his right and shot at him twice. One round hit the man's lower abdomen, causing him to tumble to the floor. He held his hands over his stomach and rolled from side to side. A younger man grabbed one of the stools. He held it overhead and ran towards Micah.

Micah shot him in the shoulder. The stool hit the man's head before falling to the floor. The man jumped into one of the booths to dodge Micah's gunfire. The truth was: Micah's magazine was already empty anyway. Micah holstered the gun, then he drew the revolver. He aimed it at Mackenzie. He heard the police sirens approaching the diner.

He shouted, "Stop! Everyone, *stop!* I can do this all day, but you don't have to die tonight. I only want *her.*"

"Then let us go!" a woman cried from under a table.

"I'll let you *all* go. All you have to do is… stand on these seats and tables."

He pointed the revolver at the booths under the storefront windows. He limped forward, causing some of the patrons to flinch and panic.

He pointed the gun at the door and said, "And one of you stand in front of there. Just stand there and… and you go home tonight."

The patrons whispered amongst themselves. *Can we trust him? Is he going to kill her? Should we let him do it? Does that make us killers? Are we going to die?* After witnessing the death of one waitress and the shooting of two men, the patrons weren't willing to fight back. The father helped his son climb onto one of the tables. His wife stood with their daughter on the neighboring booth's table, shivering and whimpering.

The other patrons reluctantly followed their lead. They stood on the tables in front of the windows. The elderly man with the newspaper stood in front of the door.

As he walked past Mackenzie, Mario said, "I'm sorry, hun."

He joined the others in front of the windows. Their eyes glimmered with hope as the police arrived. The cops cordoned off the street. Two police cruisers raced to the alley behind the building, searching for a vantage point.

Red and blue lights cycling behind him, Micah limped forward with the revolver aimed at Mackenzie's chest. Mackenzie walked backwards, limbs shaking wildly. She crashed into a stool, knocking it over, then her back hit the bar.

She stammered, "M–Mi–Micah, I–I'm sorry... I was... I never..." Her voice broke, her lips trembled, and tears dripped from her eyes with each blink. Voice raspy, she said, "I never meant to hurt you."

Micah gazed into her eyes, hypnotized by the gold flecks swimming in her green irises. He clenched his jaw as he leered at her plump, shaking lips. He ran his eyes down her body, snickering deliriously. He gulped, like a starved man at a buffet. Her breasts, barely visible through her thick shirt, aroused him. He imagined himself gripping her hips while fucking her in the doggystyle position. Despite the pain emanating from the gunshot wound on his hip, his dick became erect.

He still loved her.

He said, "Well, Mackenzie, you did. You *did* hurt me."

"I'm so sorry."

"You're just saying that because... because you're at the wrong end of this gun. If you weren't, if our positions we're flipped, you would have shot me."

"Tha–That's not true."

"It is! You don't give a damn about me! None of you ever gave a damn about us! You... You... You'd shoot me for fun—for shits and giggles. You know why? I know why, but do *you* wanna know why, Mackenzie?"

"It's not true," Mackenzie squeaked out as she lowered her head.

Micah said, "It's because manipulation is part of your nature. Women have been evil since the beginning of mankind. Look at Adam and Eve. Eve— that stupid *cunt*—was tricked into eating the forbidden fruit by the serpent. So, what does Eve do? She *tricks* Adam into eating it, too... All for her own sick pleasure. That's what *you* did to me. You tricked me into falling in love with you, then you rejected me and humiliated me in front of everyone. You went home and laughed about it, didn't you? Yeah, you did. You disgusting, heartless animal."

"Oh my God, please..."

Micah continued, "You could kill a man without batting an eyelash. You want to kill me right now, don't you? You want to shoot me, huh? I know you're trying to trick me again, you fucking whore. Those crocodile tears won't work on me. I'm not Adam, you stupid bitch. I'm Micah. I'm the second coming of the Supreme Gentleman. And I'm here to eradicate every filthy whore on this planet. I'm here to... to spark the revolution. I'm the match, you're the gasoline. Got it?"

Outside, the police formed a perimeter. They waited for the SWAT team to arrive. Four cops in the alley grabbed rifles and extra vests from their trunks. The hostages whimpered as they listened to Micah's hateful speech.

Mackenzie said, "Micah, please, I'm begging you. I– I really... Oh my God, I really didn't want to hurt you. I just wanted to be your friend."

"Fuck friends!" Micah shouted. "Do you know what I did to my 'best' friend? I killed him *and* his mom. I cut that cuck's dick off. But, before that, I fucked his mom's ass with a rolling pin. I fucked her until she bled. Then I smashed her head with a fucking frying pan. I punished her for being what she was: an old, nasty woman. And... Hey. Hey, look at me." He grabbed Mackenzie's chin and lifted her head, forcing her to look at him while smearing his blood on her jaw. Micah said, "And do you wanna know what I did to your best friend? To your... 'your sister from a different mister?' I went to the salon today. Just a few minutes ago, actually..."

"No," Mackenzie gasped, bug-eyed. "You're lying."

"No, I'm no woman, Mackenzie. I don't lie. I went there, to Lee's Nails..."

"No..."

"And I shot them. And not with this measly thing, either. I shot them with a fucking rifle. I watched gallons and gallons of blood spill out of 'em. I watched their heads *explode.* I shot Bev, that bitch, and I probably killed her sister, too. I wiped her family out. How many of your coworkers were there? Huh? How many of your friends?"

"No, no, no," Mackenzie repeated, devastated by the news.

"And let me tell you something: It felt *so* fucking good doing it. I would do it again and again and again. You wanna know something else? It's all your fault. If you didn't reject me, if you had just showed me a little respect—a *teensy* bit of human decency—this would have never happened. If you didn't lead me on, if you didn't play with me…"

"You bastard!" Mackenzie cried out.

The phone rang. A hostage negotiator was outside, trying to get in contact with Micah, while a pair of cops crouched their way into the diner through the back door. From the kitchen, they could only see Mackenzie's back. They couldn't risk exposing themselves without a clear shot. A shootout would have led to a bloodbath. The door chime rang as the mother led her daughter out through the front door. Her husband and son stayed behind, unwilling to aggravate the shooter. The old man stood his ground. He felt compelled to see the situation through to the end.

Her voice trembling, Mackenzie said, "You–You're mental…"

"No, I'm honest. I'm free. I've seen the light."

"N–No, Micah, you… you're sick. You're really sick."

"I *was* sick, but I took my medicine. I took the Black Pill, you see? I'm as healthy as can be."

"No, you're not," Mackenzie said, shaking her head slowly. "I knew it since the first time I said 'no.' You... You got so emotional and... and desperate. You couldn't take 'no' for an answer. Then you changed so quickly. You went from kind and gentle to angry and... and evil. And you only got worse, obviously. You are sick, Micah. You need to get help. You can shoot me, but it won't change anything. You're not going to start a damn revolution. There are too many good people out there. You could have been one of them. You can still change."

"What are you... No, I'm... You're trying to trick me again."

Mackenzie responded, "I'm not trying to do anything. I don't want to help you. I hate... your guts. If you really did what you said you did, then I wish you were..." She rubbed her cheeks and smiled nervously. She said, "I wish you were dead, Micah. That's the truth. But that doesn't mean someone else can't help you. Just drop the gun now and give it up. Stop with the murder and do *one* last good thing in your life."

"You hate my... No, *I* hate *your* guts. You don't really believe any of that. I can't be helped because I don't need help. You're... You're a fucking whore. You're a master manipulator and you're trying to–to manipulate me! Again!"

Micah dug his fingers into his hair and paced in front of Mackenzie. The phone and the door chime rang again. The man who was shot in the gut ran out of the diner. The other injured man whined in the booth while applying pressure to his wound.

Micah said, "You want me to give up. You want me to spare you and these people. What good does that do me? Huh? I've been mistreated by society my whole *fucking* life. I've been humiliated and beaten. The world has laughed at me. Ha! Ha! *Ha!* Those videos those kids uploaded, they got millions of views and 'likes.' It was entertainment to people like you and him and her and him and *her!* It's all fun and games until the victim fights back, isn't it? A couple of weeks ago, you were all laughing at me. Now you're crying and begging for your lives. Now you see me for what I really am: *the Alpha*."

Mackenzie said, "You're lying to yourself and you know it. You're in pain. You don't care about those names… those titles. Alphas and betas, players and 'cucks'… That's not you. You were a good person when we first met. Micah, *please*, do yourself a favor and end this. You'll go to prison, you know you deserve to be there, but at least you can get some help."

"I told you! I don't… I don't need… help…"

Micah breathed deeply through his nose as he staggered. He was lightheaded and dizzy due to the loss of blood. The color faded from his face as his vitality waned. The door chime rang again as the hostages exited the diner. The old man held the door open for them. He was ready to use himself as a human shield if Micah turned his attention to them.

But Micah paid them no mind. He stared at Mackenzie, face twisting into a grimace of pain— emotional and physical. He started to believe her. There was something about her voice that always gave her words an air of honesty. A headache stabbed his brain from every angle. He felt like his mind was being torn in two by his conscience. The 'evil' side of him wanted him to continue his genocide. The 'good' side of him asked him to drop the weapon and turn himself in.

"Should I... Should I kill myself?" Micah asked in a hushed voice.

"What?" Mackenzie responded, baffled by the question.

"They all killed themselves."

"Who are you talking about?"

Micah, face shimmering with tears and sweat, chuckled and said, "I really don't know anymore."

Mackenzie could see he was sick and suffering. She was an empath. She couldn't help but feel sorry for him.

She said, "Micah... Let's just walk out of here. You don't have to die tonight."

Micah glanced over at the booths. Everyone was gone. The old man exited the building, too. He saw the silhouettes of cops under the red and blue lights.

He sniffled and said, "Yeah, um... I guess it's... Okay, I'll follow you."

Mackenzie felt bad for him, but she was still afraid of him. She feared he would shoot her in the back. But she didn't have any other options. Part of her wanted to die anyway. She felt responsible for his massacre. His words ran through her head: *'it's all your fault.'* She walked forward with her hands up. She stepped past the tables. She trembled upon hearing Micah's first step behind her. She reached the front door before hearing his second step. She looked back at him and gasped. He aimed the revolver at her, his face knotted in a confused sneer.

She said, "Micah, please–"

Then the gunfire erupted. Mackenzie fell to her knees, wrapped her arms around her head, and shrieked. A bullet shattered the top glass pane of the door. One of the storefront windows burst. From the kitchen, the two cops rained down a hail of bullets on Micah.

Micah was shot once in the nape of his neck. The bullet went through his trapezius muscle. Another bullet hit his right shoulder, entering directly under his shoulder pad. Three bullets hit his back plate before two rounds entered the small of his back. As Micah turned around to shoot at the cops, two bullets hit his chest plate. One of those bullets penetrated the steel, the vest, and his flesh, drilling into his liver. Another round hit his thigh, which caused him to push his knees closer together and squat. Micah shot the ceiling once, then a bullet hit his head. He fell back over a table, a bloody slab of his brain hanging out of the exit wound at the back of his head. His frosted tips were now completely red—*bloody tips*.

The cops shot at him twenty times in nine seconds. Eleven of those bullets hit Micah. And seven of *those* bullets penetrated Micah's body. The headshot killed him instantaneously. Yet, with his head dangling from the edge of the table, his dim, hollow eyes were fixated on Mackenzie. Mackenzie stared back at him in disbelief. She felt droplets of his blood on her face. She lowered her shaky hands slowly, then she screamed.

The door opened behind her. Two cops dragged her out of the diner, then four cops entered the eatery with their weapons drawn, as if they were expecting Micah to resurrect himself and attack them. Mackenzie was haunted by Micah's sunken, dead eyes. She screamed until her voice broke, then she screamed some more. She was sedated at a hospital, but Micah's lifeless eyes followed her into her dreams. And, even in her nightmares, she kept screaming and screaming.

Micah's crimes were reported on the news until the entire world knew his name—*Micah Watson*. The coverage continued after he was linked to the Uber killings. His manifesto was published online by a journalist, then it was advertised by news networks around the globe. He was praised by incels across the internet while Fisher's profile was hacked and vandalized on Fuck-Less.com. His profile picture was changed to a screenshot from a pornographic video depicting a man watching his wife fuck another man. The revolution was not televised because it never happened.

The cycle remained the same: a deadly shooting, sensationalized news coverage, hundreds of questions and no answers, finger-pointing without solutions, another deadly shooting, more sensationalized news coverage…

Join the Mailing List

Did you enjoy this disturbing exploration of loneliness, entitlement, misogyny, and extremism? Interested in exploring other dark, taboo subjects with me? Are you a fan of the macabre? I regularly publish dark, disturbing, and provocative horror-thriller novels. My books blend true crime and splatterpunk to create convincing characters, to tackle unnerving subjects, and to create unforgettable experiences. I dabble in other subgenres, too—supernatural, psychological, dystopian, body horror, and so on.

If you'd like to learn more about my books and stay up to date with my latest releases, please sign up for my mailing list. By signing up, you'll also guarantee that you won't miss out on any of my huge book sales. (I'm known for offering some *blowout* deals a couple times a year.) I usually send one email a month, but you may receive two or three during busier months—or none at all if it's a slow month. Either way, I promise I won't spam you. This is strictly about my books. And it's all free! Visit this link to sign up: http://eepurl.com/bNl1CP.

Dear Reader,

Hey! As usual, thank you for reading! I expect *Lovelorn* to be an upsetting novel. It's full of extreme violence, including graphic violence against children and women, it features an ending that reflects events we've seen way too many times, and it is loaded with disturbing, hateful dialogue. Some people might misunderstand or misinterpret this novel and believe Micah is a reflection of myself. For those of you who know me—those of you who are familiar with my work—I think you know I'm more like a gentle beast. There is no hatred flowing through my veins. (except for my hatred for sexual predators.) Anyway, if you're new to my work, I hope you weren't offended. And if you were offended, I hope you didn't ignore all of my **warnings**—on the product page, in the front matter, on the back of the paperback. It's a reflection of reality, but at the end of the day, please remember: it's just a book.

Lovelorn was inspired by Joker. Yes, *that* Joker, the 2019 movie directed by Todd Philips and starring Joaquin Phoenix. I know it's the 'cool' thing to hate it, but I loved it. It was one of my favorite movies of 2019—and that was an amazing year for cinema. After watching Joker, I revisited other films with similar themes, including Taxi Driver. The troubled characters in these movies spoke to me. They told stories of mental illness, loneliness, and desperation. I've dealt with loneliness and desperation, so I wanted to tackle those subjects with this book.

At the same time, I remembered reading about the tragic death of Bianca Devins—which I recreated in a way for the first chapter of this book. I started researching her death, which led me down a rabbit hole. I read about a boy, Landen, who was thrown from a third-floor balcony at a mall. (He fortunately survived.) I read about mass shootings committed by men who felt neglected. So, I found one of my themes: *entitlement*. And I found my subject: *involuntary celibates*.

Incels.

Fiction and reality blended to create this novel. In fact, you may have noticed some scenes in this book are actually inspired by real crimes—some of which I mentioned in the previous paragraph. I debated with myself about keeping them in the book. I didn't want to come off as tasteless or heartless, but I felt like they were important for setting the tone of the book, driving the message home, and describing the beginning of Micah's radicalization. I really wanted the internet to be a big part of this novel, which is why I even went ahead and purchased the domain for www.fuck-less.com. The internet connects us to people around the world, but the lonely tend to find themselves in the darkest parts of it.

The final chapters... I wrote a school shooting scene before. I won't mention the title because I don't want to spoil that book, despite it being almost three years old. I felt uneasy about writing this scene for many reasons. But, again, I felt like it was necessary. I wanted to look at it from as many angles as possible. It wasn't about being 'epic' or 'edgy,' it was about being brutally honest and effective. I wanted it to hit hard, and I hope I succeeded.

If you enjoyed this book, I would really appreciate it if you could spare a couple of minutes and leave a review on Amazon.com. (or your local Amazon store if you're one of my international readers!) Feel free to leave a review on Goodreads, Bookbub, your blog, your vlog, or even Twitter or Facebook. Word-of-mouth is the best marketing tool for independent authors. Every review, every shoutout, and every comment leads to more readers. More readers leads to more resources, and more resources leads to more books! Of course, as I've always said, your reviews and your kind messages also motivate me to improve and to continue writing.

Need help writing your review? You can try answering questions like these: did you enjoy the story? Would you like to read another story with similar themes/characters? Was it too disturbing, just right, or not violent enough for an extreme horror book? Were you satisfied with the ending? Your review can be short and direct or long and detailed. Either way, it's very, very helpful. It might just lead someone to finding their next favorite book—or the worse book they've ever read!

I'm writing this letter on March 27, 2020. In my last letter, I mentioned that I had some *big* plans for this year. For now, those plans haven't changed. In June, I'm releasing *Do Not Disturb.* In July, I'm releasing *Bad Decisions*. In August or September, I'm releasing *Kill Wu.* After that, I'm releasing... Well, you'll just have to wait because my next projects haven't been announced yet. But I *am* working almost *every* day. The current pandemic has had a significant impact on my year. Last year, my future was bright. Hell, I'd say I was even optimistic in January and February of this year. Now... well, I'll just say that my future is full of uncertainties. For example, I got married, but I have no idea if I'll get my visa anytime soon since I was planning on moving to Japan this year. I have no idea if the borders will close for an extended period, leaving me separated from my wife. I hope we'll all get out of this alive and healthy, though. I really hope you're all doing well. Your support means more to me now than ever before—and you know I've always been grateful for your readership. Thank you very much.

If you want to read more of my work, please visit my Amazon's author page and check out my other horror novels. I'm hoping to release six to eight books this year. If things get better around the world, I might release nine or ten. I'm *always* working on something new, always looking to push the boundaries and explore more taboo subjects. I write 'human horror.' I write about the awful, *evil* things people do to each other, filled with graphic detail and raw emotion. I've also written supernatural, psychological, slasher, and body horror novels. Like I said, I'm *always* working on something. My previous book, *The Groomer,* follows a man as he attempts to defend his family from a sexual predator. According to the reviews, it's the most disturbing novel of the year. My next book, *Do Not Disturb,* turns a motel into a bloody battleground after the guests are attacked by a group of clowns. I have another book planned for the summer, too. Once again, thanks for reading.

Stay healthy! Until our next venture into the dark and disturbing,
Jon Athan

P.S. If you have any questions or comments, or if you're an aspiring author who needs *some* help, feel free to contact me directly using my business email: info@jon-athan.com. You can also contact me through Twitter @Jonny_Athan or my Facebook page. It might take me a while to get back to you, but I always try my best to respond. Thanks!

Printed in Great Britain
by Amazon

78179309R00154